BYE, BYE SOCCER

BYE, BYE SOCCER

by

EDILBERTO COUTINHO

a translation of *Maracanã, Adeus* by Wilson Loria
edited by Joe Bratcher III

HOST PUBLICATIONS, INC.
AUSTIN, TEXAS

Cover Art: Jakub Kalousek
Design and Layout: Joe W. Bratcher III

Library of Congress Catalog Number: 94-076434
ISBN: 0-924047-10-0

For

Afrânio Coutinho
Eduardo Portela
Ênio Silveira
Gilberto Mendonça Teles
Jorge Amado
Mário Camarinha da Silva
and
Moacyr Félix

*fellow fighters in
the battle for free speech*

CONTENTS

INTRODUCTION

Edilberto Coutinho is an internationally known journalist, literary critic and writer, highly praised in Brazil, Argentina, Venezuela, Cuba, France, Portugal and the United States. Since 1979 he has taught literature as visiting professor at fifteen American Universities. In 1978 he was appointed a Writer in Residence at the University of Iowa, where he had earlier participated in the prestigious international writing workshop. Besides various important Brazilian awards, in 1980 Coutinho's collection of short stories *Maracanã Adeus* (1980) was the first Brazilian book to win the *Casa de las Américas* prize in Cuba. It has been translated into Spanish and French and published in Portugal. The French translation won the coveted *Prix de la Traduction Cultura Latina*. *Bye, Bye Soccer* (1994) is the first English translation of this volume of short stories.

Bye, Bye Soccer, (*Maracanã, Adeus*) written and published during the military dictatorship in Brazil, is regarded as an example of literature of protest against the oppression and manipulation to which even sport was subject to during those turbulent times. The choice of soccer as a theme was motivated by various factors; soccer as an emblem of Brazilian popular culture, on one hand, and the soccer game as a metaphor for the complex social and political battles that took place on Brazilian soil at that time. Even though the immediate context of these short stories is Brazilian, the final message, that of determined participation in the "game" and resistance, extends beyond Brazil. The gritty style of the stories, the use of graphic, sometimes kinky images, obscenities and aggressive, often colloquial language were at that time another weapon aimed against the rulers and the strict censorship in Brazil. Fourteen years after its first publication the ninth edition of the book came out in Brazil in the Spring of 1994. The game seems to be going on. . .

The eleven short stories in *Bye, Bye Soccer* are an allusion to the eleven players on a soccer team. Each story can be regarded as a "game" of a different player and each player's story refers to a different aspect of soccer and life in Brazilian society. Coutinho mixes the characters of fictional players with the lives of real players, such as Pelé, Kempes or Garrincha, a device that adds verisimilitude to the archetype of the soccer player, regarded as a hero by society and presented by Coutinho as a struggling and often abused professional.

One of Coutinho's main concerns in this collection is to show the evolution of soccer, from an elitist pastime of the Brazilian upper class to the only means of survival for the players, who often come from the most destitute groups of the society. Another purpose of these stories is to show how the popular sport of soccer, which began as a form of entertainment, became an object of manipulation and the players became tools in the hands of the businessmen and politicians. In this sense soccer undergoes a similar process of institutional abuse and deformation as the famous Brazilian carnival. Like carnival, soccer also means for many Brazilians a way out and often the only escape from harsh reality.

Many references to various aspects of Brazilian every

day life and popular culture contribute to *Bye, Bye Soccer*'s educational value. One can learn a great deal from this book not only about the universal mechanisms behind professional sports, but also about the fascinating and unjustly, underrated Brazilian culture. The book is also regarded by critics as a literary masterpiece. Readers can enjoy Coutinho's style of narration, thrilling and sophisticated at the same time.

Elzbieta Szoka
St. Edward's University
Austin, Texas

Some people accomplish tasks,
I'm just
a snake in the grass.

— Sebastião Uchoa Leite
(in *Antilogia*)

They even pretend to respect me,
those fuck faces, but it's only
because I'm doing well now.

— Leleco in "End of an Agony"
(in this volume)

Opening Act

Lord Supreme Mathematician,
Thy power of infallible and perfect calculus come
Give us each day our daily news
about lots of goals
beautiful goals by my suffering little Bangu Soccer
Team.
Forgive my wife for being a pain in the ass
as we forgive ourselves for our stupidity when perforating
the tiny holes on the
Soccer Lotto ticket mistakenly.
Lead us not into temptation to root for another team.
Deliver us from the goals of our opponents
and bestow terrible cramps upon the shins
of their forwards.
Amen.
What now woman?

While hurriedly swallowing the watery coffee and
mentally trying to articulate his morning prayer, José Dias
da Cruz, errand boy in a Government office, hears dona
Raimunda, his wife, speaking once more about those words:
unhappy and unhappiness.

José repeats that nobody is happy, properly happy, Rai, happiness doesn't exist, we're born dead and turned into angels, Rai, you know, Rai?

Irate Rai. The office is downtown. To get there before eight o'clock, José has to get up at five and take a train and a bus. He gets back home at night, never has any money, but, if at least our soccer stars were macho, specially when they play the foreign teams. Cash, grass, those stupid players. Rai only wants to know about money, money and more money.

Dona Raimunda, toothless video-idiot (she watches soap-operas at 6, 8 and 10 P.M. Monday thru Saturday) and very practical (on Sundays, she betrays the leading soap-opera actors for the TV host and commentator Celso César, known as Cecê, with whom she is silently in love) concerning soccer matters, she only wants to know about the Soccer Lotto results, how many points, José?

He knows that there were only seven points, ah, thirteen points and happiness without having to become an angel, with only thirteen points, understand, Rai? But he was far from it, far from happiness, José was very far from it. And he is thinking of the fight during the game between Brazil and Uruguay, a team of cowards, this team of ours, they should have beaten those Uruguayans. What a shame. I'm still gonna check the ticket real good, Rai, and dona Raimunda remembers, where's the money for the girl's medicine?, the little thing's got a terrible bronchitis attack, go to the Government Pharmacy, woman, they give it for free, he doesn't hear what she says, and answers, don't bug me, woman.

Fuck. But that's it, a lot of unhappy people exist in large scale according to José, and there's a bunch of them, of course, a little less unhappy, on the verge of happiness, people who at times get twelve Lotto points correct, they're about to win, right on the edge of it. Raimunda gets too impressed, José thinks, by those things she sees on TV, and feels unhappy like nobody else because she thinks of houses with swimming pools of those women on the 6, 8, and 10 o'clock soap-operas. Rai, José thinks, sees good things for other people and bad things for herself, but it's not like that, woman, there's the good, the bad, and the so-so good side of things, we're not doing well, I know, but it could be worse, ah it could, Bangu is doing good, threatening the big teams, yes ma'am, and here comes our Championship, ah the Championship is almost as good as the thirteen points. That's it woman, take it easy, stop nagging, we're doing so-so well, hang in there a little longer and stop bugging me.

Monday, five A.M., José swallows his coffee in a hurry, dona Raimunda bugs him, eat slowly, José, and he, don't bother me, bread crumbs fall from the corner of his mouth, stop nagging and enough arguing for nothing, and he hardly gets his thick lips wet with the watery coffee (what a tasteless little coffee, this one) and leaves the house, and on the corner of the street at the newsstand, he stretches his hand to pick up a copy of *Folha Esportiva*. With the newspaper under his arm, José walks on to work. At the station, he waits for the train to come. Doesn't that stupid Rai understand anything? If I'd taken longer at breakfast and listened to her whining and whimpering and stuff, I wouldn't have gotten a copy of *Folha*, since on Monday there aren't enough copies for everybody, it sells quickly, and I had to check the Lotto results again, fuck, only seven points?, shit. Yes. It could well have been a mistake when he checked the ticket before (two times on the radio and once on TV), a mistake that could have made him jump to the heights of a demigod. And also, of course, José wanted to read the comments on the game, the game he had seen live — while listening to it on his little transistor radio glued to his ear, he had his eyes nailed to the field — and watched it again at home on the TV replay. But he still wanted to savor the best moments of the game once again, Bangu is really at it, huh, buddy, he said to an acquaintance he had bumped into at the station.

Raimunda complains about the garbage, they've brought the containers but people keep throwing the garbage all over the place; the first goal Bangu scored was a beautiful thing, like a picture, Laerte received the ball in the middle of the field on the left side, he ran to the attack, dribbled the left forward Astolfo, who backed up to block him; on a rainy day, it's so difficult to walk over the gutters, rats and garbage; fought for the ball with Bombril, wasn't blocked, and ran to the touchline; and they still call this place Villa Progress; crossed it to Nicanor who ran and chose the corner of the goal to shoot; it ought to be called Villa Retrogress. And goal on the eighteenth minute of the first half.

When Botafogo tied the game with Bangu, the errand boy José Dias da Cruz's heart almost stopped. He prayed, had faith (it's your cross in life, José), and Bangu scored the second goal. Besides the open sewer, there's the garbage from the houses up there; the second was a cross by Nicanor on the right, then there was some confusion, all the Botafogo's backs headkicking and Bangu's forward, and the ball shot up and,
the garbage comes down the gutters,
inside the penalty area on the left,   getting
everything clogged, overflowing and invading the houses,
Maninho raised the ball for João Jorge to

headkick, face to face with their goalie,

that's why the rats live as they wish, in the middle of all that garbage. And goal in the 13th minute of the second half.

Calm down, woman, everything's gonna get better, let's stay here, they're gonna build that housing project and we have our rights, Mr. Souza, he knows it all, told me that we have our rights, Rai, and we'll get a new home, but Raimunda complains that the kids are always sick, that there are so many rats around here, and besides the stench from the gutters, which makes everybody sick to their stomach, I know we're not doing well Rai, but, it's gonna get better, you'll see, woman, it's gonna get better. I know it is, hang in there.

It's 6:35 A.M. now and the sun has risen but it still looks sleepy just like José, just like almost every passenger at the Villa Progress station. Getting up a little earlier doesn't help much getting a seat on the train, there's always the struggle to get on when they open the steel animal, doors are open and there is that God-save-us-all kind of crowd, it only stops when every seat is taken and the unlucky passengers have to travel standing for almost an hour.

Straphanging with one hand, José Dias da Cruz holds the *Folha Esportiva* with the other, they didn't highlight Bangu's victory the way he expected, that's how it is with those bastards, if you root for one of the big teams, you see, even if their team loses or ties a game, they give lots of space in the paper to their team, but a small team is nothing, a small team has no voice, that little space and that's that, buddy. More people get on the train at every station, increasing the sound of the straphangers, if Nicanor played for a big team he'd already have been invited to play for the Brazilian National Team. José Dias da Cruz can feel the strong black man's body heat glued to his body, he turns and says, it ain't easy, man, and the other smiles nervously, it sucks bro', there's that 176-passenger capacity sign but there are 400 passengers or more in here, José Dias da Cruz, errand boy, calculates in his mind, they are all squeezing Christs, we travel like canned sardines, but that's how it is, a small team is nothing. That Nicanor, a real soccer star. And José repeats, it sucks.

At a quarter to eight, José gets to the office. There's the ritual of putting on the work uniform, after having punched the clock, gotten the thermos and tray. Here the only person that roots for Botafogo is Mr. Souza. José has already put on his errand boy uniform. Good guy, this Mr. Souza, and he's not a fanatic, maybe I can tease him because his team lost, your Botafogo is chicken, huh Mr. Souza? Only if he gives me the chance. The comments on last weekend's game will still be made on Tuesday or even Wednesday. Thursday is the day of great concentration, every mind in the office working on it, folks let's fill in the blanks on the Soccer Lotto tickets and José is in charge of bringing his coworker's ticket to the Soccer Lotto store on the corner every week. And there's the raffle in which everybody participates with opinions and a little money. Only poor people are lucky, says Mr. Souza's secretary, that chick from Meier with those big boobs and butt. Did you see that lucky hillbilly farmer from Mato Grosso? To a coworker, holding the sheet of paper with everybody's signatures, it's signed, Mr. Souza said the raffle is a good idea, you can tell your boss. And they just bet a little money, minimum bet, beauty Friday and Saturday are the days of great anxiety, for anybody can wake up a millionaire on Sunday. But on Saturday, a lot of people are already out, snake bit, when they announce the results of the first games.

Sunday again, José stops in Joaquim's bar, asks for a drink, throws some of it on the ground for his patron saint, and swallows the rest of it in one sip, you're leaving early?, Joaquim wants to know and José, gonna see the opening act, Joaquim, there's this boy playing real good, and looking good like a real soccer star. Well, well, tell me, pal, you're talking about this so-so blond kid of my Vasco da Gama? Well, well, no, Joaquim, it's this one who's a little bit more on the black side, Joaquim, he plays for Bangu with his kinky hair and thin skin, Joaquim, he does whatever he wants with the ball, Joaquim, he has total control of the ball at his feet, you've gotta see 'im, Joaquim.

Sunday night, dona Raimunda is infuriated with the lucky next-door neighbor. That stupid girl, Zé, they picked her in the *Luck Chest* contest on *Cecê's Show,* Zé. But José is still enjoying the feeling he felt in the afternoon: what a pity, Rai, they're not gonna show the opening act on TV, woman, you'd see it, woman, you'd see it, and that lucky woman, Zé, won a color TV, this big, Zé (Ah, Cecê was smiling when he handed her the prize, ah, Cecê looked even more handsome than Tarcisio Meira, the leading actor on the soap-opera *Demigod*), that goal was a beautiful thing to see, Rai, I even felt something inside me, and I suddenly cried, Rai (what's the point of telling her all about it?)

that stupid, stupid girl, Zé,   but I looked around
and saw other people crying, Rai,   if at least we had a
color TV, Zé,   that   kid   Bean
dribbled every player on the Fluminense team's defense, we can see those strong boys were all raised on baby formula,

all of them full of vitamins, suntanned from the beach, and that kid Bean, agile and skinny, dribbled all of them, one by one, and the audience stood in the stands, Rai, people in general admission stood on their toes, and I was crying, and they shouted, applauded for the kid, everybody, that world of people inside Maracanã Stadium, giving support to him Rai, shouting his name.

I want to know about beans in our own pans, Zé.

And everything went well, Rai

Have you asked Mr. Souza about the house again?

Because this kid Bean played the devil

We're so unhappy here, Zé.

After dribbling everybody like Garrincha,

We've got to change our life, Zé.

He scored a fantastic goal, just like Pelé, Rai,

This place is bad for our kids, all the rats, the garbage, the stink, what a dog's life, Zé,

And I cried, Rai, cried happily because we didn't deserve that much, I know we didn't right in the opening act.

ELECTORATE, OR. . .

The Rebel's Theme

The young journalist asked rapid-fire questions:

Do you know that you and your teammates also play a political role as an efficient scapegoat for your people? That you're a good campaigner for the Government? And if you guys win this World Cup, they're going to use your victory for political purposes?

I looked her real hard in the eye and said that it's difficult, Miss, not to be a campaigner for this Government and we should have nothing to do with it.

. . . or, I looked her real hard in the eye and said what's this monkey business about politics, Miss, we've got nothin' to do with it, dunno nothing, y'know? I don't get it, my business is playing soccer.

She: Do the players have only a very elementary educational background?

I told her that a player who is concerned and interested

in improving his professional status, in working with the union and things like that, is not welcome, and there's just a few of us willing to meet outside the stadiums and the owners of the teams watch us to see if we're trying to change things, calling us delinquents, cursing us on the spot, calling us kids and subversive.

. . . or, I said, that what matters, Miss, is performance on the field where the player's gotta produce, 'cause a player's got to play and it ain't for us, Miss, to discuss things like politics, and culture, and we really don't understand anythin' about that, Miss, what's important is the performance of the player and whether the players nominated for the National Team (well, not meaning to boast because I was) are really the best Brazilian players today according to the coach who's got to know it. But look at him, I said, when our goalie walked by, that guy might talk to you about this political business you want to know so much about, it looks like he's gonna run for councilman in his hometown, but she said that he was going to be councilman for the Government party and that didn't matter, and then I tried to dribble her questions again and said that the National Team is the most important thing to happen in a player's life.

She: Do you know what Brazil was like before 1964?

I said that I was nine years old in 1964, but my father had told me what Brazil was like before, that at school we only heard propaganda since they said nothing was any good before, and after 1964 everything got better, everything was running well for the country, for the people, but looking around was enough to see it wasn't true, no, so we started not to trust all the propaganda, I said yes, I knew very well that I was part of the National Team which indirectly belongs to the Government, I know it, and then she said I was an idol that annoyed the big shots politically, and I said, Miss, I can't pretend any more, it's hard, you come to me and ask questions and what am I going to do? I can't lie to you, can't deceive people any more. It would be good for them if I kept my mouth shut, but that would hurt me anyway, and I said that they keep repeating the same things to us over and over all the time so whatever they say will stick in our heads so we'll repeat them like a prayer, like a rehearsed mass, when we give interviews, but if we told everything that goes on in training camp, it would be a madhouse.

. . . or I said that I was only nine years old in 1964, Miss, dunno nothing, very little, and she insisted on asking if I was aware that I belonged to the National Team which belonged indirectly to the Government, and I said that, Miss, I'm just starting my career, and I don't wanna go through my soccer career without a goal, and it's the eve of the World Cup, the country is boiling, you know, all that expectation, and here you come to talk about politics, we better talk about soccer, or, better yet, forget about it.

She: What's a player's social life like? Is he well accepted outside the stadium?

I said that inside the stadium, of course, he is, all that world of people, all the unknown fans, the crowds, as well as, presidents, ministers, generals, all the big shots, but this meeting between the players and society Miss only takes place while the game is on, but here outside the field, it's goddamn hard, there is no. . . what is it? (She repeated: homogeneity) yes, that's it: ho-mo-ge-ne-i-ty? that you mentioned, no there's no meeting, and the differences continue to exist, oh, yes, Garrincha may have met the

President of the Republic half-naked, wearing only his shorts, but that's too little, no, I don't agree with that writer you mentioned who wrote that it is. . . how does it really go? she repeated: the victory of the barbarian Indian or the ragged Negro over the cultured super well-dressed white man. No, cut that out, I said. Bull. And I don't even see what he saw in that example you gave me about Pelé totally nude and soaped all over, being hugged by that American blond who later was murdered in his country, yeah, that story I know, everybody knows it, right? but I don't see such a meeting, as you said citing that writer whose name I can't remember, overcoming the barrier, oh, no, I don't believe it, Miss, seriously.

. . . or, I said that it's a normal life, many players are married, have children, I said, that I didn't read this thing the writer wrote about overcoming barriers, meeting, that's it, but Garrincha and Pelé, yes, I can say that Brazil owes these two great idols a lot, and our people will always have to be thankful for both of them, who did a lot for the popularization of our soccer.

She: Is whatever you say to the press criticized by the Technical Committee?

Then, the interview was published and nobody came to tell me anything about it, but I felt things could get ugly on my side, that they could even find a way to throw me off the National Team or else keep me sitting on the bench, yeah, I can see the game they were playing with me, those men on the T.C., just letting out line like when we go fishing, throwing the line with the bait, but I'm a smart fish; then the doctor major of the National Team said to me, you're a smart boy, huh? an educated and political fellow, huh? he was making fun of me, the son-of-a-gun, the way that young lady wrote about you, huh? you are good at soccer and good with ideas.

. . . or, then, the interview was published and I felt that the men on the T.C. expected that I had said some stupid thing, some nonsense, like our goalie does, then, the major doctor said to me, you're a discreet boy, huh, I liked seeing that you were not influenced by that newspaper woman, journalists are dangerous animals, they like to invent, to poison everything, we have to be careful with what we say nowadays, then he asked me how I was feeling, I said that I just had to train and keep fit, then he said that I should keep an eye on my knee and my thigh muscle, I said that everything's OK, Major; I know I'm no fool, since this son-of-a-bitch could make up something about me like I'm in no condition to play and keep me out of it, saying I need to recover from something I didn't even have, I know how it is, I really know how it is.

She: Is the repercussion of an interview, like this one, positive for the player?

Now I could see the consequences of my getting things off my chest, that I still couldn't open my big mouth, and I thought things were getting better, I said, I screwed myself up, it still wasn't the right time to, I opened my mouth too early, and there was the result, it was negative for the sport, however, it was, I know, very positive outside the club, but the thing is I couldn't stand it any more, I had to speak out, the journalists came and I said it was all right but the subject had to be soccer, just soccer, because that's what I know, but they wanted to go deep into something, I escaped from it, I dribbled their questions, I kicked their questions to the corner so to speak, and they kept thinking I was another jerk, just useful for kicking the ball on the field, a hollow man, then I thought I had to show a better image of a player, why do I have to play soccer and do nothing else? that sad and shitty life of ours and we feel like speaking out, voicing our opinions outside the stadium, and then I said a lot of things and the young lady got excited and called me the rare bird of soccer, and when she asked me why the others didn't stand their position, didn't speak out, I said, you know, we take risks, a player is pre-conditioned, we can't be romantics (yes, I was being one then) a player's a part of the machinery, but you, she said, are from a less manipulated generation of players, less a puppet,

. . . or, now I could see, even after having said so little, that the big shots are not fooling around, specially now on the eve of the World Cup, yeah, those things she published did happen, but it wasn't the right moment to speak out, if I was still a student and not a professional soccer player that'd be all right, maybe I could even answer you better, but now my only concern, young lady, has to be my profession, it's the game, I could see, even having been discreet, a player is first and foremost a player, he has to worry about his position first, his profession, I didn't please anyone, at least not totally, and there it was, the repercussion of the interview, it was negative inside and outside the team, still outside it meant nothing.

She: So, if you win the World Cup, they're going to use your victory?

She insisted on that point and she was really a fox and I didn't want to present myself as a sucker, a jerk, so I said, yes, the government is gonna use our victory, I know it very well, I've always known it, she said you're going to be the only one aware of what's going on?, since from what I know about the others, you are alone (I felt like telling her everything, pouring my heart out, and, of course, going to bed with her), the others didn't even bother about what I was saying right? if I asked any other player, if he knew he's linked to the electoral process, for example? if I said the electorate is another name for that, the correct name, of this mass of people called fans (she was talking and talking and I had it bad for her, that heat creeping up my legs) and then I said d'you think I'm gonna be alone for a long time? a new generation of soccer players is coming and. . .

   . . . or

> *Only the rebel saves the world.*
> — *André Gide*

END OF AN AGONY

The head of the young, agile, athletic Minister shone with its marvelous, voluminous black hair undeniably enlivened, thanks to the creative experiments by the one and only, talented Manolo, the big drag queen imported directly from Rambla de Las Flores of Barcelona.

His concern with the exterior appearance of his head was fundamentally important now that the country praised the outside more than what there might possibly be (or better, might not be) inside. Young, agile, and athletic, the Minister was very certain that he owed a lot — for his skyrocketing, mundane and political success — to the competent Manolo, and he always thought tenderly of that casual walk on the way to the Catalan Barrio Chino when he came across that Beauty Salon for Men, where Big Tits Manolo reigned: Miss Spanish Pageant Doll in The Palm of Majorca a year before. Since then, the young, agile, and athletic Minister had entrusted his haircut, coloring, and the other fixings of his precious hair to no one else.

Kinky-haired Leleco knew all about it. They need me, those sons-of-bitches need me, now they depend on the son of an illiterate washer-woman from Sergipe. They kiss my ass because they want to make a fortune from my

16

famous name. They need the barefoot kid, they depend on this kid's feet. After they use me, if I make a big mistake, they're going to say, go back to your place, you stinky nigger, I've got to take advantage of it while they need me, they're giving me all this support, spoiling me because they depend on me now. They even pretend to respect me, those fuck faces, but it's only because I'm doing well now. There are the others, fuck, and that's a drag, but fuck the others, I've got to get mine while I'm doing fine.

A Wise Man Among the People.

Agony is a Greek word. The root, *agon*, means the place where the athletes prepared themselves for fighting in the arena. The term degenerated to its current meaning because of the nervous tensions; the anxiety of victory that oppresses opponents on the brink of facing one another. We all know the beauty, the nobility and the greatness of sports competitions since their origin, the Olympics. In the capacity of Minister of Culture and Sports, I want to congratulate you, people. And I wish to celebrate with the whole nation the end of the agony we went through in the face of the terrible threat of seeing this unbeatable athlete, whose contract has been fought over among the greatest sport clubs in the world, leave our land. A wise man once said that destiny. . .

The Minister interrupted his Social Communications press officer's reading.

I have to leave now for a meeting with the Foreign Affairs Minister. Go on with the research. I want everything, absolutely everything about the word agony. Including its use in poetry.

In poetry? As you wish, Minister. He scribbled: in poetry. Bring me more elements for the speech tomorrow at 3:15 P.M.

Three fifteen, without a doubt, Minister.

Special Mission

All set, Leleco. You're not going as a simple soccer player but — this is what I want to propose to you among other arrangements and it's just a matter of your agreeing — you'll go as official representative of our Government and our people, our whole nation. You know, Leleco, they're going to pay us a big homage in Spain, it's already been officially ordered by Generalissimo Franco? I talked to my Foreign Affairs colleague about that yesterday. They decided to name a Santiago de Compostela street after our country. You know, brotha, there is this region called Galicia where the city of Compostela is (Brotha? The young, agile, and athletic Minister liked to use that expression which had the additional advantage of making his image more popular as his active, hopeful Social Communication press officer had stressed, but addressing a kinky haired Negro that way was in somewhat bad taste), you know, my very dear Leleco, most Spanish immigrants that come here are from Galicia. The President agreed — after he talked to our Foreign Affairs Minister — with my suggestion. You'll be appointed special ambassador representing Brazil at the inauguration of that street in Spain.

(Before everything was set and they could announce the good news on national TV that Leleco would stay, the young, agile, and athletic Minister of Culture and Sports received the player privately, behind closed doors, after having posed at his side by his office door for thirty local and foreign journalists covering the event.)

The others, right? (The Minister guesses Leleco's question.)

This guy is a sweet talker, acknowledges Leleco. He

foresaw the game, and attacked first like we do on the field. (Leleco then remembered that the President shook hands with every player after they won the General David Padilla Arancibia Cup, and he had promised them a special prize.)

Yes, I know and I'm proud of you for being concerned for your teammates. I can see that in your face, my dear Leleco. Give it some time. We have to cut the nation's expenses at this worldwide moment of crisis. We're living on a very strict cost cutting regime, Leleco. It's necessary that we go through this now so we won't have to face a wartime economy. Look, we would need to get a very high sum to buy the houses we promised the players for winning the Arancibia Cup. But a help campaign is about to be created which will allow us, my. . . my very dear Leleco, will allow us — I am sure — to help everyone, everyone. We'll launch it on TV very soon. By the way, it is my wish to have it done soon, right after we announce your decision to stay in our country.

Leleco nods yes, supportively. The young, agile and athletic Minister tells him about the special compensations he'll have as special ambassador. An errand boy comes in with coffee and mineral water.

The Minister: It's Pelé brand coffee. In my opinion, it's the best.

He hands a cup to Leleco and when the errand boy leaves: By the way, my very dear Leleco, I received a letter from your mother. (But Mother can't write, she can hardly sign her name.) I was informed that her brother, your Uncle Oscar (Ah, it was that hoodlum who wrote the letter for her, that guy should be a soccer referee, I haven't seen such a dishonest man anywhere in the world), your Uncle Oscar, my very dear Leleco, is one of the candidates running for Mayor for the Government Party in the next municipal election. Naturally, he'll have our massive support. We'll mobilize every possible resource in his favor. He's a splendid candidate — a real patriot, honest, intelligent — and I don't say that just because he's one of your relatives. I met him not long ago. But, look at the letter, a very beautiful letter, my dear Leleco, it touched me a lot, very deeply, and surely, with all due permission, we'll have it published in the papers. (I get it, Leleco thinks, once again he could see the fans turning into voters.)

A Wiseman Among the People (II)

A wiseman says that destiny exists and everything has a reason for being. The agony we all went through serves us — or will, the Minister says, serve us — to get together in this deep understanding and mutual appraisal we owe one another. Leleco today is a symbol of our struggle for the preservation of our most legitimate values.

The Minister interrupted his press officer's reading. Who's this wiseman? I can't stand inexact things.

I'm sorry, Mr. Minister. The citation was picked from a recent address by his Excellency the President and. . .

The Minister cuts in a brusque way. Well, get all the information from a qualified officer (the cruel stress on the word *qualified* is heard in a severe tone when the Minister speaks in a very poised voice) on the President's staff.

Shall do, Minister. May I continue?

The young, agile, and athletic Minister takes a deep breath and smacking his left fist on his right hand permits himself to allow the officer to continue his reading. In a very dry voice: You may.

Petitioning Christ for Your Excellency and Family

Dear Sir,

We must thank Christ for conceding us the glory of having a Government which makes thousands of families happy. I had already shed many tears just thinking of the sadness of seeing myself permanently separated from my only son, my worshipped Leleco. Then this wonderful thing happened that only you, Your Excellency, were able to do. I saw on TV the moment Your Excellency said that this was the most important matter, the country's fundamental interest: Leleco's staying in our motherland to continue giving great happiness to thousands of our compatriots when they see him play soccer so marvelously — this is God's given gift — over which Your Excellency watches zealously, always looking out for our people's welfare. Then, I shed new tears which for me were a balm of hope and, hugging my extremely dedicated brother Oscar, who has already had the honor — if not the most joyous moment in his life — to meet Your Excellency — to whom he respectfully sends his regards — along with his friends who were at this modest house (but always well frequented, since my brother Oscar is very much liked by the population of Cedro de São João), I cried and laughed with emotion, at the same time I was praying and petitioning Christ to watch over Your Excellency and Family. It was a prayer that rose from laughter and tears. A sincere prayer from an afflicted mother, already old and sick who might not have recovered from a permanent separation from her only son, who's the breadwinner of the house. Your name, sir, will go down in history, for Your Excellency understood the suffering of many parents whose children are far away. I don't know you personally (my beloved brother Oscar guarantees me that I will have this wonderful opportunity when Your Excellency comes to our little town, as promised, for his inauguration as Mayor), and I ask you for your forgiveness for taking the liberty of sending Your Excellency a big hug.

Your faithful servant,
Petrolina Maria de Conçeicão

A Brute Pain Pulls My Hair

Agony is misery, anxiety, affliction. An instant of life immediately preceding death: to go through agony. Decline, near end: The agony of a political regime. Stop, the Minister abruptly interrupted his press officer. What about in poetry?

In poetry? His press officer, after skipping a few pages (noticing he's made an error, clears his throat nervously):

In the agony of so many nightmares
A brute pain pulls my hair. . .

In an awkward gesture, the Minister pats his hair. Who's that by?

Augusto dos Anjos, sir.

The Minister seems to be meditating.

Here's one by Olavo Bilac, sir, our greatest poet, leader of the campaign for the obligatory military draft.

One of the most imminent national needs at that time, blah-blah-blah, you don't need to tell me c'mon, read it, c'mon.

The officer:

The yellowish sun sets and Nature watches
In the same solitude and at the same sad hour
The agony of the hero and the agony of the
day.

(Fucking boring. Was this Bilac a fag? Maybe Manolo will like it.) To the officer: Leave the poems here. We're not using them for the speech. Get me a short, simple, intelligent address.

And he underlined, if possible.

Goals Against the Oppressed
(Minister's Soliloquy, Adolf Hitler in Background)

Yes, the common man identified himself with that brat. That's because victory is the common man's pleasure. This wave of solidarity for this little stinky nigger, yes, because the illusion of victory is shared by more than one hundred million of the stinky and fucked. Thirty million of them can't even handle a toothbrush. Beasts that I wouldn't trade for my horses. My speech did well in the ratings, it's getting better, my image is growing, I'm making myself popular, thanks to this brat Leleco's popularity. Now we have this little nigger tied up in gold and silver chains which will keep him here, a handcuffed slave like his African grandfather, but in a different way now, Princess Isabel was crazy, everything happened because of that beast Viscount who didn't slap her with his flip-flops, he didn't have the balls to do it, that French doll, my God, where in the world have you seen people think that a nigger is a person? But what a fantastic thing this power of soccer, I have to watch that more and more closely, the public's concept of the game is really incredible. I can evaluate it well now, as possibilities, yes, the possibility of distracting the masses politically, the possibility of converting their applause at a match into acclamation for the Government. (The Minister wrote: the applause of the people at sport events can easily be transformed into acclamation for the Regime.) I have to talk privately to the President, he and I need to go to the soccer stadiums, although, he and I detest the game (oh, Manolo, we de-test, dahling, you can't imagine), the games, oh, old Adolf was so right, and that's that, now I remember that everything, every itsy-bitsy thing is in *Mein Kampf*, it really teaches you, my black buddies, Hitler gave the map of the gold mine in it, and his regime showed very well how possible it is to use sports for political purposes, oh, what a glorious thing that film about the Berlin Olympics is; yes, it's old Adolf who shows very well how to use goals scored at a match against the oppressed, it's all in there in *Mein Kampf*, in the clearest German. And what about soccer in the factories? (The Minister feverishly elaborated on the theme, his agile, long, white hand soaring like a bird writing down topics on the thin paper to take to the meeting with the President.) To those in charge, without a doubt, it is very important that spare time won't become badly oriented freedom. Yes, and in factories, and offices, everywhere, soccer can guarantee that that won't happen. Don't we call a very well-trained team a perfect machine? And it's necessary that things are kept like this; that the players be like parts of such a machine, that they let themselves be handled by a knowledgeable person. By the ones qualified to make the machine work satisfactorily. The whole thing about this brat Leleco was really good for me, it opened my eyes even wider, what fantastic potential, brotha. What's a player? (The Minister scribbled) Summing it all up, he's just like anybody else who makes his living by selling his labor, it's clear that a player should never be given the right to express his ideas on the use of that labor, it could be a dangerous thing, very subversive, oh, that's awful! (He amuses himself by making a disgusting face and raising one of his eyebrows *à la* Manolo.) Of course not, the players can't claim to have the right to decide what use their sports skill should be put to. You think it'd be funny letting this goose who laid a golden egg go to those Spanish fuck faces? The hole is a little lower, my sweet Manolo. Our forward Leleco is worth millions of pesetas? What am I saying? Of dollars? Worth of gold? Well, we're keeping the brat right here with these gold and silver handcuffs, and the extra compensation of a special ambassador and everything else we've prepared for him, you assholes. Imprisoned. There's no Princess Isabel for this little nigger, no, no certificate of freedom, no, there in Pernambuco, my grandfather knew how to deal with niggers, with old Gouveia niggers learned their lessons with a whip. But times have changed. (This asshole Count D'Eu really screwed up, maybe he didn't even fuck Isabel good, they say she did it with that nigger Zé do Patrocinio, what a terrible pun on the count's name.)

The Day Leleco said, I'll Stay

For the welfare of soccer and the happiness of all Brazilian fans, Leleco has just declared to our great Channel 12 Sports News, that he'll stay. His statement brings to every Brazilian mind the famous words uttered by Emperor Dom Pedro in 1822. (Leleco appears on the screen, and off camera, the voice of the announcer.) My life is samba and *feijoada*. I'll stay. Those were, ladies and gentlemen, the actual words from our extraordinary Leleco. He'll continue to show his soccer star's classy and fine technique on our nation's soccer fields, raising our beloved country's sports legend to an international level. After these messages, dear viewers, stay tuned for the soap-opera *The Adventurer's Son* by Jane D. Black, while you wait for new, sensational revelations about the happy ending of this lively controversy. Our Minister of Culture and Sports has even said that this is the end of a long agony, which shook our nation, this international turmoil we can say, about the widely known contract offered Leleco by an international team. But with millions, offered first by the Italian and then by the Spanish team, in his hands — the last proposal by the Spanish was truly a multimillion-dollar deal — our soccer star, resisting the temptation of the vile metal, now responds with his patriotic and magnificent I'll stay. For the welfare of our soccer and for the happiness of the Brazilian fans, Leleco said he'd stay. (On the screen, concluding the interruption of the Great Sports News, quick cuts of Leleco playing, showing his short dribbles, goals and, especially, his violent kicks which make him a great soccer idol.)

Love in the Afternoon

He: Shameless big ass.
She: Stinky nigger.
He: Slut. Hooker. Whore.
She: Son-of-a-bitch. Faggot. Gutter mind.
He: Plaft! (He slaps her a good one)
She: Fuckface. Fuckface. Fuckface.
He: Plaft! Plaft! Plaft!
She: Shitty nigger.
He: Disgusting white trash.
She: Stick that yummy black dick up my ass.
He: Here it comes, my whole dick. Turn your big ass around.
She: Tear me all up, honey.

Half an hour later they left the motel. Leleco knew how to spank well, without hurting. Maria das Dores got a very delicate, little kiss on the cheek from the soccer player when they said good-bye. Oh, said Leleco raising his left wrist, reading his watch, my holy dick, it's almost five. The taping. It's about to start. Taxi, taxi. I'll call you the day after tomorrow, princess. Take care, my black one. You too, princess.

Goals Against the Oppressed
(Ordinary Man in the Bar)

He's a real nice person.

With his eyes glued to the screen (Leleco's interview on the day of I'll Stay) João Jorge Gomes, an ordinary clerk at the branch post office in Meier, Rio de Janeiro, with a missing front tooth, a fanatic rooter for Flamengo (a member of the *Flatal* fan club) turned to the black woman at his side, at the bar, and asked: Don't you think he's a nice person? And while she answered, he gulped down a glass of nice, white cachaça.

Golcawelso is Born

Dear viewers, we have here the famous journalist I. Habib, social columnist of the newspaper *The Universe*, who at this moment will officially launch — along with the distinguished wife of our Minister of Culture and Sports — the Golden Campaign for the Welfare of Soccer. In her capacity as honorary president of Golcawelso, founded on the single notion we should never forget to mention, a brilliant and timely idea by journalist I. Habib, Mrs. Maria Helena do Prado Gouveia, first lady of Brazilian Culture and Sports will now speak on this show exclusively.

Dona Helena, a little plump, almost neckless, live, nationwide and in color, walks shyly to the center of the stage where the *High Level Show* is being presented: Well (Nervous giggles), well, dear friends of Channel 12, more important than (she's about the pee in her panties, a strong emotional response) words, uh?. . . (the press officer asked her to try speaking in a colloquial tone, at ease, didn't he?) real important, uh? (before the mirror while Manolo does his hair, the young, agile, and athletic Minister makes a severe judgement about his wife: colloquial but not stupid, you whining, dumb, goofy, fat, jerk, imbecile). Finally, the woman manages to say that more important is the gesture and then (gleaming in her light pink dress created by Vicente Campos, our splendid fashion designer as the most widely read columnist I. Habib would write the following day) taking her wedding ring off her left hand, she places it on a tray which the social events columnist is holding firmly.

I also want to follow the example, says I. Habib, with perfect ease before the cameras. He passes the tray to the host of the *High Level Show* and takes his heavy bracelet off his right wrist. He shows it to the camera in close up and places it on the tray noisily. He makes his trademark *V* sign with the dignified emphasis of a winner of all the battles old Churchill might have imagined, with blood, sperm and yelling. And he says, while the camera focuses on the gesture of the index and middle fingers of his hairy right hand: a wise horse never goes downstairs. Now that you're all updated, my dear lady viewers, on everything about Golcawelso, you may all go to bed for that revitalizing little beauty rest so you can wake up well disposed for horseback riding lessons tomorrow. (Horseback riding was in fashion, widely known to be Minister Gouveia's favorite sport, the columnist I. Habib sees very high political possibilities through him.) Now, you may turn off the TV 'cause from here I go on. . . But do not forget, my dahlings, we need gold, much more gold for the welfare of our soccer. It is our people's response to the advances of the liras and pesetas which are threatening our Little Canary National Soccer Team. We'll fortify our regal sport with this campaign, giving our most notable national soccer stars the means to stay in the country which they love so much, defending our triumphant colors.

Channel 12 programming is over after a commercial showing Leleco running around a track, volleying, headkicking the ball, and finally getting close to the camera, saying that he takes *Tonic V* every day to keep fit.

Announcer's voice off camera: V for Vitality. The Tonic for the strong, the winners in all walks of life.

Of Selling One's Labor

While he dials the phone Leleco keeps thinking, she's just like me, she lives on the product of her labor. She can't choose. Like me. We're all slaves to money. But who isn't? They sell my contract; she sells herself. Life's a big fucking whore house. But who's not into it? Even the good-looking Minister, all dressed up and perfumed, is also into it, no matter how hard he tries not to show it. On the other end of the line, someone answers.

Maria das Dores isn't home? (He was going to call her the following day, but all of a sudden he felt that uncontrollable lust that could only be satisfied by jerking off or coming in the ass of a small freckled white woman.)

Mad for her. No sir, Maria das Dores gets home at six. All right. This is Leleco. Tell Maria das Dores to give me a buzz. Yes, she's got my number. He puts the receiver on the hook. The national circle of prostitution was closed. Only Maria das Dores assumed what she was, but everybody, in reality, everybody had his price, nobody was free. He kicked a stone with sudden anger. But who isn't? Everybody's a slave. Leleco thought, everybody's fucked in this fucking life. But that's what it is: the game's gotta go on. Now, with his conscience a little lighter, he walks on the wide avenue by the sea. On the sidewalk, he stops and stares at a boy who's flying a kite. That's cool, the soccer superstar concludes, because flying a kite makes the kid get used to looking up and up. And that's fucking cool.

VADICO

He chested the ball, bringing it down to his foot willingly and unleashed a shot into the net and goal. Yes, says the television announcer, he was a soccer superstar. Watch these scenes, dear viewers. Dangerous foul. Vadico takes some distance. Just a few steps back. And look at that. When he ran towards the ball, the crowd sang oooooooh, which ended like an explosion inside the stadium. That game was in Paris. Billboards in the street read:

GO TO THE PARK DES PRINCES
SEE PELÉ AND COMPANY

This stadium has the ideal type of grass for playing soccer. Princes' Park, Paris. Yes, sir. The grass is compact, you can fall on the ground without hurting yourself. Of course, the stadium that made the biggest impression on my life was Maracanã, and the most beautiful I ever knew was Wembley in England. But I can't forget the French fans' tenderness and how nice it was to play on that flawless, well-kept grass, a wonderful carpet, really, reminisces Vadico.

Pelé and company. The teammates. Just Pelé and Vadico were worth the price of admission. After the usual applause for *King* Pelé, the crowd had a good time with Vadico's kicking. The French loved and idolized Vadico. *Est-ce que cet homme a cent pieds*? The One Hundred Footed Man. That's how his nickname was born.

The One Hundred Footed Man, in the show, after that game in France, shows his scar-covered shins. They demonstrate, says the commentator, the characteristic violence of the backs he faced.

The One Hundred Footed man, an idol, a soccer genius. Being interviewed, Vadico says, no, sir, I wouldn't trade my soccer career for anything. The scars? He examines them. The commentator says, they are like a sour prize for being hit hundreds of times.

Couldn't he blame life?

Anyway, I can't tell a story in an organized way.

The game is on. On the TV screen, the same commentator:

Where are the idols of yesteryear? Most of them are forgotten, lonely, abandoned. How do they live? What do they do? We found the famous Vadico, the great striker who played so brilliantly at Pelé's side, sitting on a park bench, sad and lonely, looking at least twenty years older than his actual age.

While my second coffee gets cold, I see everything again on the TV in the bar. They repeat the show about Vadico's career. I sat here and asked for coffee with bread and butter. Dunking the bread in the coffee, I ate everything quickly. Then, I asked for a second cup. I drank it slowly. Now it's already a bit cold. Doesn't matter. I really asked for the second to have the right — so the Portuguese waiter wouldn't bother me — to stay at the counter a little longer. 'Til the end of the program.

Body in the air, back to the goal posts, a scissors kick on the ball. An anthological goal — bicycle kick — proving that Vadico should really be included among the greatest soccer heroes, beside Leonidas, Garrincha and Pelé, says the commentator. Let's watch it again, announces the off-camera voice. The replay is shown. In that match, Vadico might have kissed the grass once a minute. But, it doesn't matter. Let's follow it dear viewers. He gets up from the ground in a jump (he looks as if he were made of rubber) and is ready again for combat. And when the opponent (the film's narrator goes on) thinks he has dominated him, Vadico takes a horizontal position, stretching his feet like an arrow in the air. In this position like a hurt animal, he does (watch it closely, viewers) an incredible series of scissors kicks (the video shows him in slow motion now), receiving the ball in the center from Pelé (this is still during the game at Princes' Park) and kicks the ball turning his back to the net.

When Vadico scored a goal like that, you would think you were dreaming, you needed to rub your eyes. The French said, after seeing him playing his devilish game beside Pelé and Garrincha, that Brazilian soccer was sheer black magic.

It's in black and white, this *Fantastic Show Of Life* (that's the name of the show, in color, with that cute young woman at the beginning showing her little well-shaved armpits). I'm a lost old man in this shitty life, a cataract in one of my eyes. It seems as if the whole world has become a dark room. Every afternoon, I sit on one of those park benches that the film shows. Vadico's life, huh? So much glory and now this misery of his, just like me, living like a bum. There's a statue in this park, that I can only see well in bright daylight. It's the body of a young woman (it looks like the daring young woman on the TV show) and, as evening falls, her body becomes more and more like a monster, and I go back to my room. A retired man advised me not to walk around at night and I'm still waiting for welfare to send me to the hospital for my right eye.

An old man is a dead burden, I said to the man at my side, that same day in the park. I saw him as he came closer and sat beside me. A dark beret, a yellowed T-shirt under a flower-patterned shirt (torn?), a pair of worn-out cashmere pants and rubber-soled soldier boots clothed his figure. That's what Vadico looked like when I met him. He even told me some of those stories which I couldn't believe. Storytelling is an old folk's pastime. Then I saw on TV that everything was true.

On a rainy afternoon in São Paulo (the well-dressed TV commentator's voice) his soccer career was over. He wasn't a player to give in. He had a career of more than twelve years, a striker of famous attacks. He played with Garrincha, Pelé, Gerson. Vadico never ran away from combat. In these scenes, dear viewers, pay attention, he sees the ball coming in the air, he jumps before the back. He gets the ball (the film shows) but he falls on his knee. Vadico remains motionless, in pain.

In a quick check-up, the team's doctor guaranteed that it wasn't very serious. The crack player only needed a few days to recover. But those days turned out to be the worst days of his life. A month later, surgery was scheduled. Treatment with injections and exercises hadn't worked.

A kid stopped at the door of the bar, looked at me and shouted that an old man smells like a horse. I raised my arm, in a threatening gesture, but very weak and slow, and the little devil still repeated like a horse, a horse, a horse and left running.

The Portuguese waiter smiled, it seems to me that he smiled, but why should I be bothered by that smart ass? I focus my eyes carefully to see what happened to Vadico. But now, on TV, they're showing a commercial. *To Success, with Hollywood.* This dark-skinned little woman got close to me, all agitated, her eye-lashes smeared with blue mascara — lighting up my *Continental, National Preference* cigarette — and wearing no other make up on her tense face. What will the girl order?, asks the Portuguee. That man was swell, she says, looking at the TV set. She asks for a Dreher cognac.

Two months after the surgery, continues the TV narrator, very little had changed. The star player's knee still kept hurting and the leg was motionless, despite all the exercises. Time passed for him, whose only happiness was reminiscing about glorious days. Then Vadico is shown, the Vadico I met, a rejected old man like me (however, he is much younger than me):
I lived to net goals. There were so many that I lost track counting them. I only know there were a lot. It's a pity those days are gone.
Next, we don't see Vadico any more, but we hear his voice while he's shown in action: kicking, dribbling, volleying. Then, a series of goals. A real painting, a beautiful thing to see. A picture.

At times, says the commentator, his courage cost him months on end of work. The fans wanted his constant presence. They kept giving me hope, says Vadico, until the day the team doctor came in and finally let me know: You can't play anymore. For your own benefit, the doctor told me. You'd better put an end to your career now. Yes, the doctor confirmed, the injury can get worse to the point that it will leave you a cripple. By then my knee had already been mutilated by all those injections and surgeries. It hurt when I walked or moved my leg. I understood, it was impossible to fight it. I had to stop. I have to be brave, I thought.

Another cognac, asked the little women, the voice trembled and I saw that she must have been crying, her face was in deplorable state.

It really was a tremendous act of courage, says the narrator of Vadico's life , that allowed him to get into the goal area in spite of the defender's kicks. Then — after his injury — he still had the courage to abandon all that was his life and had given him so many past glories until it left him crippled.

First, it was the violent kick from behind, on my calf. That fullback was a very stout guy (that's Vadico's voice in the film), strong as a horse. Bad player, of course. I saw that it was easy to beat him to the ball and couldn't resist dribbling. The audience applauded, shouted my name. I did not volley (the film shows Vadico controlling the ball on his left foot without letting it fall many times, a very brilliant series of volleys) and the audience roared. They shout my name louder. The films shows the whole Maracanã Stadium in unison: VA-DI-CO, VAA-DII-COO. That guy wasn't humble, proceeded Vadico. I know it, every player is horrified to let others make a fool of him. Because besides the dribbling and the volleys, he'll also be laughed at by the teammates, the public.

He was handsome, huh? says the woman taking a long sip of her cognac, tremendously handsome, a hell of a hunk.

Of course, continues Vadico, a player who runs straight to block an opponent — a forward, midfielder, or back — always takes the risk of being dribbled, like a fool. It's a risk that proves he's dedicated to the team and not a personal humiliation. But personal humiliation was what that defender felt. Adiel, that's his name. He disappeared. Don't know where he is today, an old man like me, another one that is lost out there (the voice is lower and it's difficult to hear Vadico speaking), another one who's been sent out of life. But that's it (we can hear better now), on the blocking maneuver, the first player has to be exposed to dribbling. If he gets the ball, that's all right. If he is dribbled, he can get mad and even lose his temper, like that huge back Adiel. That's when we fought over the ball and my leg didn't respond.

The little woman noisily puts the glass down on the counter:

Life sucks.

Three days ago I met Vadico for the last time. I saw you on TV, I said happily when he approached me on the park bench. I was having coffee and saw everything on TV. A lot of people saw it.

Storytelling is an old folk's pastime, Vadico said.

I don't know how to say it right, but that's what I tell everyone. They're repeating the film and I'm drinking coffee again, and watching it again and there's this woman who's already gulped down four cognacs, she's drunk and can't stop crying. They're repeating the film because of what Vadico did yesterday. (If this drunken bitch stopped having a fit I'd feel a lot better, but she's right: life sucks.)

The only memento that he tenderly keeps, says the

handsome young fellow on TV (that one, of course, doesn't smell like an old horse) is this ball (the ball fills the TV screen) and Vadico, interviewed in his little, clean room, says this was the ball I kicked that gave our team the Tri Championship. I remember it well. No sooner had the referee blown the whistle to end the match, I hugged this doll and said, it's mine, and it is with me to this day.

I wake up very early, Vadico says right afterwards, and I go out to the street which is always a little deserted. There are only a few losers who go to work at the break of dawn or some people who partied all night. There isn't much to do, young man, the same thing every day, always the same old thing. We look for what to say about people walking by or what's in the newspapers during the day at the park (that's when the film shows him sitting on the park bench; Vadico is seen alone from the distance and a few children walk past him looking with disgust at his figure, leaning against the bench). Women, young man? When Soccer was over, they were gone too. Yes, there were some of them, but it seems that I wasn't good at dealing with the, no, (a little forced smile that becomes an ugly face) yeah well, with the sluts I fell on my face. And the woman at the bar almost shouting: One more, fuck. The Portuguee brings the bottle and she: Shoot. The waiter turns the bottle and pours. The liquid slides drop by drop and the woman impatient: Do it right. Do it right. She grabs the man's hand, pouring more: like that. It's OK up there. And gulps down the new dose, half of the glass.

Today Vadico is news in every newspaper and there's this woman who doesn't stop drinking and crying. You had to get screwed up, right, Vadico? With women like this one, beside me, what could you expect, buddy? And now it's the end of the show that they repeated entirely because yesterday, as the young man is saying on TV now, the famous One Hundred Footed Man freed himself with his own hands.

It was the first thing I saw today, the headlines in the newspapers which are pegged down on the newsstands: the news that Vadico, the famous idol of old times, the One Hundred Footed Man, God of the Stadiums, killed himself by slashing his throat with a razor.

As soon as the film was over, I paid the check and got up to leave. That's when the woman raised her head from the counter, pushing the cognac glass aside in an awkward gesture at the same time she opened her hand and let go of a little bottle, without the cap, from which a little green tablet rolled. Only one. The others, the poor bitch had swallowed with the cognac.

GOT AN EXPLANATION, DOC?

All that, Doc — trips to the moon, literature, soccer. A loan our Government was going to give the U.S. A big mess, see? Imagine that, Doc. I dreamed of all that stuff for Brazil. That'd be good, wouldn't it? Well, so the country would get back on the track soon.

Pause. He starts to speak again, willing to be precise.

And tourism. Ah, he also talked about tourism. It's difficult, under these circumstances, for us to remember everything clearly, right? But I think I remember it well. Including the date and my friend's name in New York.

Rio de Janeiro

Dear Steve:

I don't know why, but when I received your letter today I thought of Pelove.

You know what I'm talking about?

It's been a long, long time, yes. But I can't forget Pelé crying out love, love, love to the world via Warner. Pelé, man. Got it?

And our Government, then poorer than yours is now, contributed this huge amount of dough, half a million dollars to warm up the party. Those jerks and smartasses from the tourist agencies, which don't exist any more (the jerks don't either, of course), brought an enormous photograph of Rio de Janeiro Bay to New York, which was displayed in a dark corridor of your subway. That cost a fortune. Meanwhile the director of one of those rundown companies said in an interview that tourism was something to be cultivated among friends. Then, he took advantage of Pelé's coming back to Brazil and threw the King a new party, gathering a very big group of friends, including various foreigners who came here all expenses paid. Minimum cost of twenty thousand dollars each. The kind of luxury nobody can bad-mouth. Hundreds of people received invitations. Deluxe invitations, printed on expensive cards with the Republic seal and everything. The sumptuous Presidential stamp was embossed. You did some research on that era in Brazil and you know how wasting money was rigorously — officially, I mean — prohibited by the Government which capriciously overused the word austerity. And there was official condemnation (ha-ha-ha) of those so-called luxuries. Remember? Of course not, the director of that tourist agency was not arrested and not pressured to leave his job. You think that's weird? But can't you remember how picturesque this country was and that's why your compatriots enjoyed it down here so much?

Well, Steve. I kept thinking of those days unwillingly.

Oh, yes. Maybe it was your ambassador's interview in yesterday's paper that made me see the picture of so many years ago so clearly. It seems our government is still going to give the United States a big loan this year. The ambassador talks about this player of yours who's going to have his contract sold in gold (at that time, we used to say in dollars) to our Brazilian pro soccer. Yeah, we are really in need of a little injection since our soccer is anemic these days.

Now, I wanted to talk about another subject. That's what I've already told you. You know, even when it was a novelty, I didn't want to go on your space shuttle. I'm sorry, but I think the idea is deadly boring. I am the same guy. You may remember that even in the 60s or 70s, when you guys were the so-called godly astronauts, I was not interested in the subject.

But what I really remembered clearly today was the day Pelé bid farewell. I also wanted to explain about the author you want to bring back to life. No, Steve. He did not write during the time you think he did. Look, he wrote the text you've just read in 1977. You say that although his ideas are old-fashioned for the twentieth century, thinking he had written a decade before São Paulo Modern Art Week (1922, right), the language appealed to you. In fact, it was curious. We read that, disagreeing with those ideas, but the angry conservative man wrote gracefully. A good choice of yours, Steve. Some of the most savory expressions he copied from nineteenth century Portuguese writers. He principally sucked straight out of Eça de Queirós.

But back to the day Pelé made his farewell. I've never forgotten that gigantic electronic billboard at Giants Stadium, on and off reflecting the final words of the King's speech: Love, love, love. And although we knew that everything had been carefully prepared, with those letters blinking and everything else, there was this TV commentator who praised, listen to this, Pelé's improvised speech. Then, during the broadcast one of those guys from tourism came on screen to inaugurate the photo display of Rio in the old Grand Central, inviting who knows who to come and see it, yes, the original in person.

Yes, there were some things you could die for. Like the guy (another TV commentator or another tour agency director?) who said that Pelé's beautiful smile had an aphrodisiac appeal for every woman on the planet. Then, an acquaintance of mine made a funny comment that when all that shouting at the end of Pelé's speech — that thing about love, love, love — could be understood as multinational monkey business, in big style under the sponsorship of Warner Bros. with institutional support from Brazil.

That's all for today. Hugs.

All that, Doc. Isn't that really weird? I remember word by word about all those things. Including my friend's name in New York. However, beside the fact that I am not used to writing letters, I've never had a friend in New York, a city that I don't know except from watching Kojak. Under the circumstances (I was unconscious for a long, long time after I was run over, wasn't I?), I think it's strange that it crossed my mind (unconsciously, right?) a subject like tourism which I don't even care about (I think it's just one more predatory activity the way it's being done, like part of the national paraphernalia). Literature, you're right. I've always enjoyed it. I am lazy about writing even a single letter as I told you, but I cultivate the habit of reading, believe me. And soccer, yeah, soccer is also right because the game is the only exit for the hoPeléssness we live in, isn't that right, Doc? Now I wanted an explanation of how all these things came up at the same time and I remembered everything so well afterwards.

Got an explanation, Doc?

Grown-up's Game

Mr. Agenor Macedo's there inside the net. What now, Mom? I shoulda asked to leave the field when I scored against our team. Nelci is only one year older than me, but he's already playing a grown-up's game. My goal. Josemar, what now?

. You're giving a few corners freely to the other teams, I know. What's up buddy? Remember what I've told ya. You gotta be cool. Face to face with the goalie, you kick right there on the angle very slowly. (Josemar made the gesture swinging his body, his right leg moving forward, imitating a player who kicks the ball slowly.)

Don't wanna know. I'm sick of it. Sick of it. Understand? I am sick of you. Enough. Where's the apartment in Copacabana? And the savings account for Dema's education? I've never seen the account. Those scenes, Mom screaming at Mr. Macedo. Mr. Macedo thought he could solve everything with a little money: Try to get by with this for a while. Mr. Macedo takes a wad of

43

bills out of his deep pants pocket, which he counts fast, wetting the tip of his fingers with spit.

Face to face with the goalie, I missed the already scored goal. The whole team came over to me. I was on the ground holding my ankle. I was hurting. It was my teammates that came over to me. I thought one of them was going to help me get up. They all gathered around me, calling me all kinds of names, they kicked me and I only raised my hand to my face, ashamed. It wasn't even to shield myself, it was real shame, and they kept kicking me. Mr. Fasano finally realized what was going on and came to help me. He was over there near the field, beside his barbecue pit, with a sausage on the spit. He came slowly shaking his fat belly and took me off the field. Then he ordered Nelci to go in. Off the field, beside Mr. Fasano, I saw Nelci dribble everybody on the other team and quickly score a goal. Then another one. Two great goals that settled the score of that game.

Hello, princess. Come 'n' honor us, the man said (one of Mr. Macedo's hitmen) and took my mother by the arm. The Samba School's rehearsal was going to start. Xangô da Mangueira was there on the stand, near the band and said into the microphone with a hoarse voice that he didn't wear a poker face, no, no, no, and Mr. Macedo tapped his fingers on the table, near a lot a beer bottles, some were full, others were half empty. When Xangô finished his song, Mr. Macedo's hitman went up onto the stand and said into the microphone that our rehearsal was going to be taped by Italian TV. He asked everybody to do his best to show a good image of Brazil abroad. He said a lot of stuff, people applauded him. He got off the stand, and went back to stand beside Mr. Macedo. Josemar looked at the directors' table and angrily beat on his instrument (a big drum) while my mother accepted a glass of beer from Mr. Macedo.

Fallen at the edge of the field, rolling over with pain, I was making an effort not to cry and I heard Mr. Fasano say to Bira: You all went crazy? Who did that to the kid? And Bira, answering the coach: Nobody did, Mr. Fasano. On the field, it was Bira who ordered, screamed, coordinated the moves, while Mr. Fasano only stared from far away, watching. He hurt himself, Mr. Fasano. Bira got closer to me and poker-faced said: Didn't you Dema?

Lying in bed, compresses prepared by Mom on my ankle, I hear her talking to one of her friends, Dona Isa, who said, I stopped in to see my Carnival costume. Mom said that work on it was really delayed, the stores in the suburbs were worthless, and she needed to buy I don't know what and she couldn't find it. She had to go to one of the stores in Copa. Mom went crazy for Copacabana. For her, good things only existed in Copacabana. For you, said Dona Isa, it's not a problem. You've got loads of it, you can buy wherever you want. Silence. After a little while, she continued: Look, you've got a good life. Why should you get yourself into a mess with this penniless man? Then she said a lot of things against Josemar and praised Mr. Macedo highly. Leave the certain for the uncertain? Where have you seen such stupidity? She said that Mr. Macedo was the one who bossed everyone around, ran the Samba School, the numbers game, our little soccer team, everything, even Josemar, because Josemar collected the money for the numbers game, so he was also one of his employees. Then, Mom said: I don't know what you're talking about all those things for. No. And her friend, Dona Isa: Yesterday, during Samba School rehearsal, he was eating you up with his eyes. Watch out. Lots of people noticed that.

Nobody's gonna stop you, my son. Go for it and be a top scorer. Mom leaves the room after she puts fresh compresses on my ankle and I hear Mr. Macedo's voice, talking to her in the living-room: How's the kid doing, huh? Mom: Much better. His ankle's still a little swollen, but soon with some herbal compresses he'll get over it. Fasano wants to sub someone named Nelci for Dema. D'you know who he is? A kid who came on the team when Dema got hurt. It's me who's talking Cida, (I can hear Mr. Macedo's voice loud and clear), I'll take care of Fasano. He's mine. No prob.

Mom was dancing in the middle of the crowd in the Samba School's rehearsal when Josemar left his place in the band and approached her right in front of everybody. I saw him pushing Mom to a corner and I saw them kissing. Mom looked around and saw me. She went back to the dance floor and continued to dance. Josemar tapped me on the shoulder and returned to the stand. That friend of Mom's, Dona Isa, was watching closely. To me, she's a hooker. Mom's gotta be careful.

I recovered and Mr. Fasano put me on the team. Bira, in the role of captain of the team, mouthing off: Taking out Nelci, Mr. Fasano? He's gotta come in and play. Fasano: Dema needs everybody's support. Soccer is everybody united. One for all and all for one. Looking humble, Nelci said nothing. I went onto the field. Fat Clown, Bira still said. Mr. Fasano pretended he didn't hear. Then, Mr. Fasano called Nelci and said: Look, kid, don't get annoyed, there's this man from Vasco who's a good friend of mine. I asked him to give ya a chance. You're going to train in Vasco da Gama next week. Thanks, Mr. Fasano.

I ran into Josemar who was collecting money for the numbers game next to the newsstand. People are short of dough these days, right?, he said to the Italian news vendor when I got closer. He invited me for a soda and took me to a bar where he told a few of his friends, this is my promising fella, pointing at me, any day now he'll make it playing for the Dearest Team. And he sang loudly:

> *I would be deeply disappointed*
> *If Flamengo didn't exist in this world.*

I don't wanna know about it. All bull. Still stuck in this shack and d'you know when Dema and I are going to live in Zona Sul? D'you wanna know when I'm going to get the keys to that apartment in Copacabana? On the Day of Saint Never. Never. Never. Mom was mad as a hornet at Mr. Macedo and because of their fight they didn't even realize I had come in. I saw Mr. Macedo touching Mom's face, running his fingers through her hair, she stepped back a few steps, I don't wanna know, look, the kid's here, she had finally seen me and Mr. Macedo left, pissed.

Look, man, that one is Josemar's chick. See how sexy she is? People say he's getting her a house. Bira pointed at the black woman who walked by swinging her hips and continued talking and looking at me. Did you know that's Josemar's woman, Dema? I said: I didn't know it. He: No? What d'you know? Tell us. You can't know nothing, man. You're always out of it. The others laughed. Bira continued speaking louder: That one, Josemar's chick, can even make a saint climb down off the altar. A real sexy chick. Then, me: You never went out with a woman. You're putting on a show, man. And she's not Josemar's woman, no. That's not the one he likes. Bira: How do you know? And then who does he like? Me: Ask'im, then. Bira: If you know it, why can't you tell us? Me: Hey, because it's him who's gotta tell ya.

I was sitting on the stoop of our house when I saw Josemar coming down the street. Then I stood up to meet him and I hadn't even taken a few steps when Mr. Macedo's car came up at high speed. It stopped right there. Then a gunshot and then more. Mr. Macedo's hitman jumped outta the car, pulled up Josemar's head by his hair and, putting his gun inside my friend's mouth, pulled the trigger for one last shot. He dropped the body on the sidewalk, went back to the car quickly, slammed the door and the car screeched its wheels turning the corner not far from there. I rushed to where Josemar was and held his head with both hands. It hung softly.

Mom angrily pushed her Carnival costume to the side and leaned against the sewing machine crying loudly. Two friends of hers came in, one of them was Dona Isa who hugged Mom, running her fingers through Mom's hair. I went to the bathroom and stayed in the shower a long time, still dressed, the water washing down my body stained with Josemar's blood which got thinner and thinner and it was the same water mixed with blood that rained on my face, and I was crying, crying a lot, but nobody could hear me.

Mr. Fasano was preparing a barbecue on the edge of the field. Our team scored the first goal. Bira shouted enthusiastically: Let's score a lot of goals. Soon after, the ball shot and came to me. A sure goal. I missed the goal post. I heard people booing me and I saw my teammates' angry faces. I saw Mr. Macedo arriving. Soon: Their goal. One to one. I saw Nelci warming up. But Mr. Fasano asked him to sit on the bench again after he received a message Mr. Macedo's hitman had whispered in his ear, the same hitman who had shot Josemar, the same who had taken my Mom by the arm to sit at Mr. Macedo's table at the Samba School's rehearsal.

Their whole team was on our side of the field. I ran back to help our defenders and I got unlucky and scored a goal against our team. Then, a crowd of my teammates gathered around me and I backed away, frightened, because I thought they were all going to beat me up again. Walking towards the edge of the field I saw Mr. Macedo coming down the stands to join the group. The game stopped. Suddenly I remembered Mr. Macedo handing the wad of bills to Mom and the blood all over Josemar, it was as if I was watching everything again. And their shouts again, my teammates' curses. Then I ran to Mr. Fasano's barbecue pit, grabbed a spit with two little pieces of meat on it and rushed back in to the goal post where Mr. Macedo was screaming at the others, saying it was not his fault, he didn't do it on purpose, defending me. I walked toward

Mr. Macedo and the others opened the circle forming sort
of a corridor. Face to face, Mr. Macedo and me, and all of
a sudden, he said, what's up, kid? Eye to eye. What's the
story, Dema? Eh, eh, eh, he looks crazy. Hey, you guys
can't anybody move? Then I grabbed the spit firmly and
stabbed it deep into Mr. Agenor Macedo's chest. He walked
backwards slowly, step by step, and fell inside our goal
post, hugging the net.

BLACK SHIP

The hand of the proud man, extended. My God, what a shame. Has Dad gone crazy? The wrinkled, flushed facial expression, the man takes a while to draw his hand back. His hand stayed out and he only suspended the gesture when my father, with a poised voice, said excuse-me, sir, for not shaking your hand, Mr. Lira, I've got a terrible cold today. The man drew his hand back and seeing me in the corner of the room, a little bit behind him and Dad asked, are you ready, Paulinho, the plane leaves in only three hours? But we have to stop by the club before that, I said, I am going to get my suitcase, sir, and left for my room.

Dad. Dad, it's recording. Gonna interview you, I said putting the microphone up to his face, he backed his head away a little, take that out of my face, kid, but I insisted. I want to inaugurate my tape recorder with you. I arrived with my brand new tape recorder under my arm, very happily, I want the first tape on this beauty to be an interview with you, and I'll be the reporter. Attention, recording, attention to the testimony of Paulo dos Santos, Paulão, to his son Paulo dos Santos Junior, Paulinho, both

51

soccer players and by the way, we belong to a family of players, starting with the renowned Edson dos Santos, my father's brother, therefore my uncle, not meaning to boast, dear listeners. I'm speaking about the fabulous soccer player Edson Marinheiro, who was, was what? Help me Dad. Dad: Who was a famous, envied center-forward. Me: In the distant past of soccer in Rio de Janeiro, Brazil.

Paulão's son, former player for Bangu (in the 30s and 40s), Paulinho told us he owes a lot to his father, whom he learned to admire, although, he had suffered some pressure to choose another profession. Leafing through the pages of a photo album: My father always let me play soccer, Paulinho told us, but he followed my development at school attentively, and if the grades were not good, he used to tell me to quit soccer. But I managed to dribble the old man and did both things relatively successfully. When he felt I could succeed being a player, when he saw I had some talent, it was he who supported me the most. Now, he thinks I play just like Uncle Edson, who my old man modestly considers to be the big star in the family. It's all right now, but in he beginning it was difficult.

Mr. Paulo dos Santos, tell this modest reporter what soccer was really like when you started. OK, Dad said, here we go, you fake reporter, c'mon daddy, you don't need to insult a modest and honest professional. Dad said, but ain't it better to start talking about brother Edson? All right, I said. Dad cleared his throat, lets go then, when your uncle started, soccer was the sport of the rich, that's what our sport was, consequently it was elitist and racist. So when Rogaciano Alves Leite, one of the most distinguished members of America Soccer Club, asked your uncle to join the club, he created an embarrassing situation. Wait, Dad, we better introduce these folks. Uncle Edson's story is the following: born in the small village of Angelina, which is not even on the map, near Garanhuns, Pernambuco, born to a mother who was a slave and a Portuguese father, left his work on the land — the Master of those lands' hoe in his hand — to be a sailor. The sea was his salvation. A marine officer, who was a friend of that distinguished member of the America Club Dad mentioned, brought him to play soccer in Rio de Janeiro, and some time later Uncle Edson brought Dad, who was still a kid, here's when my mother's voice is heard on the tape, you two want a little coffee over there?

Mr. Lira was waiting for me in the living room. I even seemed to hear the cavernous silence between him and my father, staring at each other. I was dawdling in the room. I was already homesick. The album. I didn't even think of bringing it along with me. Dad had organized all those newspaper clippings, it all belonged to him and Mom, there it was, my picture getting out of the taxi, the day I presented myself to the team, on the eve of leaving to play for the Young Champ's World Cup. And what do they say 'bout me? Among all the players, Paulinho was the most elegant in the presentation at the Hotel Nacional. Dressing in an impeccable white suit (three piece), a black shirt with white patterns and polished chrome shoes, he got out of the taxi smiling and was certain that his presence would be crucial on the National Amateur Team which would fight for the World Championship in Italy.

I quickly took a sip of fresh coffee, warm and delicious coffee that only Mom knows how to make and I said, now it's your turn to talk Mr. Paulão, speak, Dad, what was this embarrassing situation? Well, Edson was a former sailor, and besides that he was a mulatto, his skin was pretty dark. Like me, I said, isn't Mom always saying I look very much like him? And you remind me of him when you're playing, Dad said, you two resemble each other on the field, more than you and me. I've always said that, and it's funny because you never saw your uncle play. But when I'm playing, Dad, don't I look like you a little? You look more like him, which is good, because he was a real soccer star, a great player. You were also great, I remember you, hungry to play a full-blooded center forward, a tiger breaking up the opponent's defensive wall, all those things they wrote about you and they were all true. But enough with the compliments, kid, you want me to talk or what? I've never seen such a crazy reporter.

I really played quite well, a flawless game, the gringos put me on the clouds. I brought all those newspaper clippings from Europe for the album Dad was putting together, then Dad said, soon you'll have to think about renewing your contract, you can't play with these things, the big shots don't play. The big shots, no, I said, smiling, but let it be, we'll get everything straight. Then I asked Dad if he wanted to be my manager, my representative to resolve all those things with the team, and he said no, soccerwise he only wanted to see me playing, and from far away, on TV, his heart was too weak to face the pressure cooker of Maracanã.

Well, your uncle's acceptance in the club was going to harm the fashionable elitism of that time. Dad pauses, takes one more sip of coffee. But the refusal would certainly cause great embarrassment to the person who had proposed him. Rogaciano Alves Leite, I said into microphone, interrupting Dad, as well as to the person who'd be accepted, Dad said, my Uncle Edson, I added, being nosy. I liked hearing the alternating sounds of dad's voice and mine speaking about Uncle Edson. Dad repeated that Rogaciano was a celebrity in the club, a big shot, I said, well, Dad said, he really bossed everybody around, I know, I said, he bossed everybody around, he was one of the big shots of that time. Then, I said, to butter up Rogaciano they found a way and Uncle Edson finally joined the rich people's club. The first black player on the team to be a member of the greatest club. America never became a great team, Dad said, but all the clubs at that time belonged to the rich, and then Mom came over to us, took her glasses off and with her near-sighted eyes she made a funny face and said boooooooooo, a crazy, unexpected thing, and we three laughed, in good humor, and she picked up the coffee cups.

With the Argentines, it was easy, they set up a defense the way I like, in a line with one player in the back, I can walk away with the game, it can be their National Team, Amateurs or their big stars, it can be the River, the Boca, if it was all up to me, all of our opponents would be Argentine teams so I could score a lot of goals against them, and those three goals I scored in the final game were my consecration, and like a bonus I passed the ball to Geraldinho who scored a goal, we won 4 to 2 and we won the Young Champs World Cup easily. I came back home proud, with the international title. Mom kissed me and I saw that Dad was damned touched.

Yeah, they found a way to fix things, but it was like war. I remember that one newspaper at that time published something like a true crisis in the ranks of the club on Rua Campos Sales, it was the *Imparcial*, which called itself the morning paper that covered sports in Rio de Janeiro the best, and it had a very good journalist, my father said, who signed his name Dangerous. He was a very daring man, Dangerous, very outspoken, and it was he who started to fight bravely, had a lot of guts, his pen only knew how to blacken the paper by praising Edson Marinheiro. The thing got worse and the *Imparcial* published that a group of more than sixty club members would leave the club, headed by Eusébio Lira, who is Mr. Lira Junior's father, the one I know, right? Dad said, yes, and at this point the phone rang, and it was him, Eusébio Lira Junior. (Yes, that group of sixty racists quit the America Club).

Yes, you can speak. On the other end of the line, Lira Junior asked me if I could stop by at the club, he had a very urgent matter to discuss and guaranteed, it's a good thing for you, Paulinho, but I'd rather not anticipate anything on the phone. I've already talked to your lawyer, Lira Junior said, but the lawyer didn't tell me anything, I asked him to come here and we three are going to have a meeting. Lira Junior set the time (in two hours). I wasn't that happy, but I didn't want to show that to Dad. I went back to the tape recorder, let's go on with your testimony, Dad.

Yes, Eusébio Lira organized a protest, with a petition and everything else, and then with the group of dissidents, joined the Fluminense Soccer Club. Part of that group were the Curtis brothers, the Dias Lins, the Azevedos, the Maias. I interrupted, Dad, how can it be that you're so sure of all those names after so many years? Very sure. Our friend Dangerous, at the *Imparcial*, Dad said, continued to oppose the elitism. He published the headline:

EDSON MARINHEIRO INCLUDED
ON AMERICA'S FIRST TEAM

and on the same page was the news of the protest. Then
there was retaliation. That's when the team was going to
play a friendly game against Tupinambá of Juiz de Fora.
Although brother Edson's name was on the list of players,
at the last minute, he was benched. But Uncle Edson was
still on the starting team? Yes, he was. Oh, man. That
Uncle Edson was really hard on the fall, huh? Really hard.
He had to be. He stayed and took part in the Initium
Tournament.

He was the star of the Rio de Janeiro Championship
for years running. But, at the nomination for the Brazilian
National Team, they used to forget about him. They praised
him to his face. Behind his back they used to say he was
pedantic, conceited. A little nigger that didn't know his
place, they bad-mouthed him.

Then that's how it is, Oliveira said, from father to son,
the inheritance of dreams is forged, a whole family of
great players. Well, I signed with Oliveira and he became
my manager. Yes, the dream, but I know that since my
father's time, since before my Uncle Edson's time, there's
been no real change. The same short-lived glory, deceitful,
and for the few, while we help people, the world of people,
at the stadiums, forget the oppression they live under, or
like Oliveira says, to alleviate their tensions, he says it's
the cathartic function of soccer, very important, it's true,
he says in a tone of voice that we don't know if it is this

function of soccer that is very important or if it is his words, because he's one of those people that put on a real show when they speak, they like to hear their own voices, stressing the words well. Oliveira seems to be about to make fun of what he says, an essential cathartic activity, he keeps saying. I know, but for me that means I'm being used like they used Uncle Edson and Dad, then Oliveira is also gonna show up at the club for that meeting, Mr. Lira Junior and him, let's go see what's gonna happen.

What's the Initium Tournament, Dad? An Initial Tournament, c'mon. All the teams that participated in it were to play the championship in games that lasted only a few minutes. Well, brother Edson, I say imitating the sports commentator, the phenomenal Edson Ma-ri-nhei-ro, well, your Uncle Edson was one of the greatest stars, he scored eight goals that afternoon, he had the devil in his body, brother Edson, and Dangerous did not spare praises about him in the *Imparcial*. Now, you talk about yourself, Dad.

On the neighbor's radio, Roberto Carlos is screaming in his samba-bolero style that I came back, came back to stay, I came back to the things I'd left behind, here's my place, but soon I have to say good-bye, bless me, Mom, bless me, Dad, while barking, a dog smiled at me, we have no dog, I came back, I cried, Roberto, go on samba-bolero singing, they're going to send me on the Black Ship, don't do that to me, Dad, I've never seen you so mad, that doesn't look like you, you're not like that, no, Mom, can't you say anything, can't you do anything funny to make us smile?

About me? What d'you wanna know, you fake reporter? Easy, Mr. Paulo dos Santos, more respect to the written, spoken and teleguided press, I mean televised. How was it when you started, Dad? Was there real professional soccer? No, not yet. It was a time they called brown amateurism. And, in the 30s when I started, blacks were already accepted without a problem, at least on the field. But prejudice existed, it kept existing, and it was felt even in the way people, who said they were on our side, spoke, like that Colonel Barbosa, who thought he was dignifying the Bangu players, calling us, get this, little pinky mulattos, my little pinky mulattos, he said. Son-of-a. . ., I said. What? No, nothing, Dad. Say it. A reporter who's afraid of words is no good. Isn't it rude? Of course not, what's that nonsense now? Then go to the kitchen, Mom, and you explode on the tape recorder: Son of a bitch, that shitty Barbosa. Dad, laughing: You said it, buddy. Son-of-a. . ., huh? That's it, like that.

Mr. Oliveira here is in agreement, Mr. Lira Junior keeps saying, and for you Paulinho it's gonna be a good opportunity. Ribeirão Preto is a very friendly town, it has a distinguished university, you'll be able to continue medical school without a problem and it'll be only, it'll be only, I suddenly don't hear what he's saying, anyway they had already set everything for me, without consulting me, and they came and tapped me on the shoulder. Oliveira's shoulder, Mr. Lira Junior's, and I only thought of Dad, how he'd react to that. What was Uncle Edson's style like, Dad? He played like you, he liked to struggle in difficult games, really hard ones. The tough matches didn't frighten him, they motivated him even more. I know, everybody knows that it's not fun and games with me. I'm the kinda player who takes risks, goes for every move, and I fight for every ball.

Ah, there's something I want to make a point of remembering, this thing about racism. There was a little march song that was kind of our vengeance, it was like all the blacks taking vengeance, on the refrain of that little Carnival march song that I remember, if I am not mistaken by the Valença brothers and Lamartine Babo, we'll check that later, I am not very sure, but it said something like you can't catch the skin color. Yes, bro' Edson shone, in spite of everything, in spite of being repelled by narrow minded whites who considered themselves owners of our soccer, and as Dangerous would write in the *Imparcial*, he was the most frightening center forward in Rio at that time, he had the guts to break up the most solid defensive walls, he was not afraid of ugly faces and superbly dummied the backs with his unbelievable dribbling. Now I see you Paulinho, and it feels like I'm watching him play again.

The black ship is out there waiting for you, kid, out there, out there, out there. Mom wrinkles up her eyes, Dad pretends to be strong with that brusque way of talking which is so unusual, Mr. Lira Junior's big black car, that black ship waiting for me, who said there was an Aurea Law for a soccer player like there was for the slaves? We are still subject to the fans' switching teams, to the management of our teams, now they've decided that they'd better sell me. The team is good, it's scoring many goals, Mr. Lira Junior said, at the moment we can allow ourselves to trade a player with your features, and we've got Tata, he said, then I said, I understand, Mr. Lira Junior, Tata is a great teammate and I want him to be OK. Oliveira agreed with everything, you're going to make your name bigger in Ribeirão Preto, Paulinho.

You talked about teleguided press didn't you? But, I was just kidding, Dad, we have to respect the Fourth Estate. OK, but d'you remember that TV show we saw last month? Yes, I said, the one about the World Cup in 1938 in France, yes, I remember. That one, Dad said. But they almost didn't say anything about the World Cup in 1930 and 1934, when we screwed up. That's true, I said, really screwed up. Well, Dad said, Brazil started badly. And they wanted to forbid blacks to be on the team. They had been forced to swallow the presence of Fausto in 1930 and Leônidas in 1934 because they were fabulous players. But, look, it wasn't easy. Tell us about when you retired, old man, was it still a big problem? Yes the problem existed, and I got to know about a secret report, you know what it's like, secret but everybody knew about it, a report that circulated around, talking people out of nominating black players for the National Team, because they would feel inferior to the Europeans. My name was being mentioned for nomination, but all of a sudden, I was sure they were not going to nominate me, then I decided to get out of there before they got to abuse me. See, Paulinho, the Uruguayans already had a black player, José Andrade, on their team which had been champion in the 1924 Olympics, bi-champion in 1928 and World Champion in '30. There's a picture of Andrade's here at home, he's hugging your Uncle Edson. Two top-notch players. José Leandro Andrade, a great idol.

It was the first time I saw my father turndown a handshake, he, an extremely black man, I mean, polite man, that's not it, I'm very confused, a black man extremely father, I came back for all those things, Roberto Carlos screams, his face flushed with anger, his face all wrinkled up, Mr. Lira, the son-of-a-bitch, I mean, son of that big

shot who wanted to block Uncle Edson. Dad avoided
telling me that, he didn't want to interfere with my career,
not to be nosy, maybe he might have even thought that
there was a bigger change since his time, since much
before Uncle Edson's time, now that hostile man, I am
sorry I'm not shaking your hand, Mr. Lira Junior. I came to
my room, kept browsing through the album, dawdling,
now it's my father who came into the room, telling me, go,
go now, don't dawdle 'cause your owner is waiting for
you, I had never seen Dad speak so angrily, don't do that,
Dad, he repeats, go, your black ship is at the door, now it's
me saying bless me, Dad, and bless me, Mom.

Dad, looking hard, Mom, almost crying, biting her lips
trying not to cry, tightening her little near-sighted eyes,
now I'm leaving, head down, just hoping that nothing will
happen to Dad's heart, now I am getting on the big ship, I
mean, Mr. Lira Junior's car, this black car that a black
chauffeur in a uniform and cap drives for the Director of
the Fluminense Soccer Club of Rio de Janeiro, who is
selling this merchandise that is me, me, extremely black
and a very polite son.

FEET CELEBRATION

The lady had physical caprices
She was a strange creature
— Manuel Bandeira

The biography of feet, that's what Olga desired.

Her warty husband (on top of his left foot there was this big wart, obscenely prominent, which he insisted on keeping, it doesn't bother me, let it be, my angel), the retired Colonel and avid reader of Olavo Bilac, had come to cover the Argentine Cup for the *Marching Letters* newspaper.

Olga took off her clothes. Naked and alone in her hotel room in Buenos Aires, she felt growing, with undeniable warmth, the desire for Mario Alberto Kempes' feet.

In his first article, on the eve of Brazil's lamentable debut, Colonel Cornélio Bandeira, the warty one, swollen by youthful, patriotic feelings, dared to write a title using a well-loved stanza:

THE GREATNESS OF OUR LAND,
YOU BRING US

He really hesitated for a while about the correct spelling

of greatness, with one *s* or two. Fortunately (a forewarned colonel is forearmed) he had at hand, not a dictionary, but a brochure by his favorite writer from the Parnassian literary movement. Cornélio tried not to be mistaken.

He's six-feet tall. At 23 (he's going to be 24 next month), he's an idol not only in Argentina but in Spain, where he was the best goal scorer playing for Valencia this season. When he signed a contract with the Spanish team two years ago the Argentine Soccer Association was careful to include in his contract a clause that guaranteed he'd be available to play for his country in this World Cup.

While Olga had to be content with what she could see about the athlete (*ay, pendejo mio*) on what we call the small screen (she follows fanatically all the televised reports), Cornélio Bandeira, the warty, Bilaquian one, kept looking for material for new articles in which he could highlight the fantastic performance of the extraordinary *troika* of professional Brazilian soccer. He didn't miss a chance to repeat that, for me, gentlemen, it's secure and refreshing and we must enjoy seeing our soccer commanded by three distinguished celebrities from the highly regarded Armed Forces of our beloved country.

Then, he formed, pleasantly drooling, his meager team of star players, composed of dignified representatives from the Navy, who (would anyone know in Buenos Aires?) hold the reins of destiny of the highest entity of our sport (the colonel found that word very noble and sonorous, and repeated *sport, our noble sport*), from the Air Force, the competent and discreet supervisor of the Canary National Team, and from the Army, a no less competent and brilliant coach at work.

Bandeira liked to refer, on the other hand, to what he called the decisive psychological factor. Gentlemen, we've been world champions three times, and the opponents, glancing over the glorious conquests from our past, on the brave campaigns in Sweden (1958), Chile (1962) and Mexico (1970), shall tremble from head to toe. All that, he stated firmly, counted a lot. The players? Don't we have superstar players? For Cornélio Bandeira (a condescending smile, twitching the left corner of his mouth), the players didn't count so much. Look, he declared, after all, it's enough for these kids to follow in the edifying examples of sacrifice, selflessness, dedication and, summarizing, gentlemen, in one phrase, love for country, like the love felt by an admiral, a colonel, a captain, so everything goes well, everything works out. And respect, gentlemen, our logistics. Everything was planned with scientific precision. We have a perfect tactical scheme. Everything's gonna work like a very well-oiled machine. Everything. He who lives shall see.

Coach Menotti said more than once that he wouldn't rely upon, to form his team, any Argentine soccer star playing for a foreign team, and such a player would be at his disposal only at the last minute. When Mario Alberto Kempes was only released by Valencia three weeks before the beginning of the Cup, Menotti explained why he'd made an exception saying that Kempes had previous experience with the National Team. In reality, he was the first soccer star to be included on the ambitious and powerful team Argentina started to form right after the 1974 Cup in Germany. The 25 million Argentine supporters are grateful to Menotti for that exception.

Kempes, on the tube. Why can't they give some miserable information about the idol's feet? Aren't feet exactly the most important things a soccer player has, his main working tool? They give all the information you can think of, fuck!, no they don't tell how many veins are on his dick, they don't. And what about his feet? Who knows what shoe size the *pendejo* wears? Soccer shoe 43, my furry one? His feet. Olga desired his feet passionately, she lusted for his feet.

Although he became famous for being a notable scorer, Mario Alberto Kempes is an extremely versatile player. He can play on the left side as well as on the right, center-forward and midfielder. During the 90 minutes, he's able to cover a vast area of the field, helping on defense, organizing the intermediary line, passing the ball to his teammates and shooting to the goal.

Pendejo, ay my furry one, feed me, cover me all over with your huge, lustful, sweet nourishing feet, your feet that organize the moves and shoot on the field. Humiliate me, step on me. Make me feel like a little ball, *pendejo*, kick me, my furry one. Kill me, wrinkle me, tear me up. *Ay, pendejo,* let me kiss your toes one by one, let me bite your big toe, softly, my furry one, *ay*, very, very softly. Yes, said the warty, Bilaquian colonel, we can be the champions perfectly. They say we don't have the great stars from the past, but that's proven to be sheer stupidity.

Deaf to the sonorous battery of criticism against the National Team, Cornélio Bandeira assured, these detractors are gonna see how our tactics will work. Sure those things take some time. But our kids are already playing well together, it will soon be incontestably solid. We'll make use of our punch, darling, we'll show the strength of our soccer, my angel. That's what counts today. May we have trust, dear Olga (he pressed his hands together feverishly), may we have trust. Pray, darling, pray. That thing about superstar players is out of fashion, sweet Olga darling (he had to tell her that, because people ran away from him in the hotel hall, whenever they saw him, they ran away from the bore). Out of fashion, as modern people say. Soccer is association, a unity of action. The Go-For-It kind of crowds will work again. Only the bad patriots refuse to join the crowd. Pack of communists. Bums. It's an absurdity, my saintly one, there are a few players that get confused with the National Anthem's words. Can you imagine that?

Argentina has the same number of points Brazil has, but the average of goals is inferior, and it will depend on the result of Brazil against Poland for the Argentinians to know how many goals we have to score against the Peruvians.

Olga is lying in bed. Naked, she caresses her breasts and brings her hand down to her navel. The TV report shows Kempes running on the field during training, and her hand going down, darling, my darling, let me take your soccer shoes off, and the hand itself making love to the soccer star, let me grab your shoe, kiss its inside, and the hand moving faster, index finger on fire, surely made out of leather smelling like a young animal. Come, little horsey. I'm your angry mare, mount your mare, my stallion. I want to rub the leather of your soccer shoe, *pendejo,* on my snout. Then I want to penetrate it with my lips as if I were a crazy mare. With my tongue, trespass this sacred place, the shrine of your feet (my angel, we'll win), feel the tepid tenderness of this niche (in spite of the spoil-sports), I want to devour you, drink all of you, my wild colt (players that don't know the words of the National Anthem well). Olga talked to the picture she had torn from the paper which showed Coach Menotti about to direct his attention to his star player's feet.

In the picture Kempes' left hand is touching his ankle. He himself puts on an ice pack under the coach's watchful eyes. For her, his ankle is the hottest in the world. She caresses, as in a dream, the perfect arch of the sublime feet that are showing. Only one, really, the other is hidden inside the shoe which is on the grass, while his owner talks to Coach Menotti, Kempes applies the ice pack. Olga rolls over in bed holding the newspaper, caresses her breasts with the photo, brings her hand down to her belly again, a moan, a panic shrivelling, her hand reaching her sex on fire.

A tranquilizing piece of news for the whole Argentine nation: Mario Alberto Kempes only hurt himself slightly during yesterday's training. A simple dislocation, a small sprain. Nothing serious, really. At this moment, in the 1,065,189 square miles of this country, one can't imagine anything more exasperating than seeing the great idol out of the Cup's final game. For the whole of Argentina, nothing is more important today than Kempes' physical condition. By the way, a coworker in the sports editorial room told us that if all of a sudden the supply of meat, wheat, lumber, corn, and fruits ran out, the people in this country wouldn't even notice the loss of these well-known riches, as long as no evil might befall the Nation's Favorite Son, Mario Alberto Kempes, the big star of 1978's World Cup.

Always Parnassian-like in love with his capricious, beautiful woman (second wife, almost 20 years younger than he) Cornélio Bandeira repeated soberly, (he didn't drink alcoholic beverages) or something like that, without any remorse:

Maybe I was dreaming when I saw her

And on their first night in Buenos Aires, on their second honeymoon (as he insistently considered that trip to be), he pointed to a handful of stars, up there, and recited Bilac once more:

There they are, all of them
filling up the sky, from corner to corner

Sick, sick and tired. She was starting to hate poetry and the Go-For-It crowds. In other words, Olga was hoping, really, at that point, that the Brazilian team would get screwed up once and for all.

When she heard Bilac again, she asked Bandeira.

When are you going to get up the guts to remove those warts, Cornélio?

The colonel tried to calm her petulance, but delicately and without losing his grip.

Feet are not a pleasant-smelling topic of conversation, my angel.

Look, Olga commented in a nicely literary way, feet are in everything, including poetry. Didn't we learn that the foot is a rhythmic unit used to divide a stanza?

Cornélio Bandeira looked at her astounded.

Look, the woman went on triumphantly, your great Bilac should have been an expert on that.

Cornélio hesitated. He was taken aback. He was the intellectual in the family, right? Woman still stamped her feet on the floor. At the last minute she had thrown in the suitcase (she wanted to bring any book just in case she got too bored) a copy of *Dom Casmurro*. She showed it to Cornélio who was dumbfounded.

Look at this line: *At my very own feet.*

Olga loved that expression. To the Bilaquian, warty colonel, she pointed out the line by Machado de Assis which read: *He greeted me, sat at my own feet, talked about the moon and the ministers.*

Cornélio was trying to think about his next article for *Marching Letters* and could not pay much attention to his wife's foolishness. Soccer as a factor for the union among nations could be the theme. It sounded appropriate to him. If he got a photo of Argentina's President-General beside the Brazilian Sports Confederation's President-Admiral, he would easily get the thrill of a front-page byline, oh yes. But wasn't it dangerous to allow Olga to dedicate herself to literature that way? An inadequate text could eventually fall into her hands. Very young, inexperienced and without a solid intellectual formation so to speak, the poor thing would have difficulty choosing. That's it. I truly need to help her choose her reading without running the risk of making a mistake. She should only read selected authors with rigorous scrutiny. He would show her (yes, that's it) how to separate the wheat from the chaff. As to this Machado (*wasn't he black?*) it wouldn't be right to compare him to an intellectual in the category of Olavo Bilac, who not only was an unsurpassable poet (*The Prince of Brazilian Poets, right?*), but also a great patriot, devoted body and soul to the obligatory military draft, one of the most imperative Brazilian necessities at that time.

In the game against Poland, on June 14, the goalkeeper Fillol was completely out of position, Mario Kempes saved

a sure goal by punching the Polish forward in the face.
Fillol defended the consequent penalty and it was Kempes
who scored two winning goals (2 to 0 for Argentina).

When the suffering Poles also lost to Brazil, Cornélio
Bandeira's enthusiasm reached the most unrestrained
euphoria.

It's our glorious march towards the title. Nobody will
hold down Brazil. Nobody.

He dully repeated with his episodic memory the slogan
which official propaganda had put in everybody's mouths
in 1970. Olga said no thank you when he asked her if she
wanted to go shopping.

C'mon, my angel, the *peso* is low, he still insisted
pushing her to go.

His angel knew it precisely. It's only 0.0012 of a
dollar, isn't it, colonel?

Olga knew she could have as many dollars as she
wanted. Her colonel had a soft heart in terms of money.
For years on end, a faithful informant gave him a hint
when the *cruzeiro* was going to be devalued once more,
and Cornélio would buy valuable dollars in time. But Olga
wasn't into wasting money now. She had calmed her crazy
shopping mania. She wasn't attracted to the knick-knacks
from Calle Florida any more, which these days was crowded
with Brazilians who were flattered to their face by
salesmen, but ridiculed behind their back, being called
little monkeys, Indians, ignorant, sub-race and ill-bred.

You go, the woman said firmly. I'll stay here.

As you wish, Bandeira gave in.

His angel's caprice was hard to understand, to come to
Buenos Aires and confine herself to a hotel room.

And before the colonel insisted:
I want to rest, she added.

In this week's retrospective, new sensational moments by the great idol of the '78 Cup. In the game between Argentina and Peru, on Wednesday, the Argentines knew that they needed to win by at least four goals to be assured of the title after the annoying victory of Brazil against Poland: 3 to 1. Kempes scored the first goal. An impeccable, irrefutable goal which gave the nervous team some immediate confidence. He also scored a surprising total of six points which will remain in the history of soccer.

After all, we'll go back home without the title, Cornélio Bandeira commented, (less ashamed than what we could have expected, Olga thought) but honored.

Moral championship? The woman could hardly keep from laughing mockingly. It was too much. She didn't understand anything about soccer, but she could laugh at the foolishness of the whole thing. She saw the whole joke. The sad truth, the warty one continued, is that the Peruvians really threw the game. Therefore, the coach of the Brazilian National Team was right, really damn right, when he claimed for the national colors a moral championship.

And after all (Cornélio Bandeira, a bit nervous, marched from one side of the room to the other), after all, my little angel (Olga, naked, fixed her hair before the dressing table mirror), after all, angel, there are various considerations to be made (a new article on marching?) on the fringe of a simple soccer dispute among nations. Undoubtedly, the Argentine people today form a united, happy family, which will not listen to troublemakers and detractors of the law and order imposed on the country by the government.

Government and people fortunately (the article was definitely taking shape in his mind) sealed their union with that victory. Olga rubbed her hand on her pussy and rubbed it on his nose. He inhaled deliciously. This is good for the continent, my darling and there it is. We need to think, at this moment, in continental terms. Brazil won't keep the World Cup Trophy this time. But it won't leave South America. Cornélio then told Olga about the magnificent Honor Tribune in the final game (it was a pity you were not feeling well, my little angel, you weren't there to see it). The present triumvirate formed by General Videla, Admiral Massera and Brigadier General Agosti, surrounded by other Argentine authorities and from various friendly nations at that great moment of intense emotion and warm fraternity. My darling. My little angel, bear that in your lovely mind. That 0 x 0 didn't humiliate us. We tied the game with the home team and, for almost everybody, it was the best team in the Cup. That was how it was considered by the competent observers, the most competent of all. We didn't lose. We didn't.

After so many nights of insomnia, the Brazilian coach could go to bed without Menotti's mockery: I congratulate the Brazilians for the Moral Championship. I hope he'll congratulate the Argentine coach for the title won on the field. Truthfully, my dear viewers, the History of the World Cup is not written by the defeated, but by winning teams.

Lying on her stomach on top of him, Olga now has her face on her husband's feet. She kisses every toe on his left foot, one by one, bites the big toe, first very softly, then a little bit harder. Bandeira complains with a little afflicted cry which he vaguely tries to conceal. She chooses the most prominent wart and starts sucking and biting the warty protuberance, which has always made her profoundly disgusted. The colonel, troubled, tries to pull her upwards. Come, angel. She doesn't stop and goes on biting it a little bit harder, now harder, as if she were to bite his toes off, holding his warty foot firmly, hard and harder and harder.

> *From the chest, the final cry is expelled.*
> — *Olavo Bilac*

NAKED KING

Ah, Nini, you're too dumb.
And whoever is that dumb, he's gotta ask
God to kill him and take him to the devil.
— The Liberated Woman of the Penthouse

You know, Brotha'll take the
best out of it. The King knows it all.
— Colonel, the Cosmos' new star

And when we're all dead,
will there be a thorough explanation?
— Nini Wonder

You can't fool me, white folks.
— Pelé

Best Out of It

When asked how his teammate, the King, was going to get away from all of that, and if he really believed there was a plot against the life of the most renowned soccer player of all time, the robust fullback Colonel (Eduardo Silva, 29), the Cosmos' new star, said humbly that, you know, Brotha'll take the best out of it. He added that, in his opinion, there might be a misunderstanding in this whole story, that soon everything will be explained. He calls his famous friend Brotha or the King. The King knows it all. Let it be, buddy, he'll always be the greatest, the untouchable idol of all soccer crowds. They want to get him involved, but everything will be explained. That Nini Wonder? No, never heard of him. Those women, over there in Rio de Janeiro? I may have met them, the soccer star admits. There are so many female fans who follow the players as if they were making them in the field, and Brotha, everybody knows, is more than a star. He's a King. Colonel reported that he intends to retire in two, three years but he won't quit soccer, he thinks he'll start a new career as a sports commentator. After having accepted a contract with the Cosmos, he quit school as a communications student at a university in the Bonsucesso neighborhood of Rio de Janeiro. Here in New York, he rented an apartment, sharing the expenses with the Italian soccer star Aldo Brancaleone, also a new acquisition of the Cosmos, who had bought his contract from Lazio of Rome. Colonel was recommended to the American champion team by the King himself. He has just signed a million dollar contract with the club. According to Eddie Firmani, now his coach, he will be one of the greatest soccer attractions in the United States next season. Although a defense player, he became one of the best goal scorers in the Brazilian championship last year with his unstopable, powerful kicks. That, thanks to the countless goals made through foul kicks, many of them at great distance. He kicked 34 penalties without missing a single one. He's going to debut playing for the Cosmos next week during a friendly game against Varzim of Portugal.

Liberated Woman of the Penthouse

Cigarette between her fingers, she points out a picture of the King in an article in *People* magazine.

Someone gave him my number. He called me and in the middle of the conversation he asked me if I had a friend who was available. Yes, I have Admiral, I said. He thought it was funny? What? Are you making fun of me? I explained to him I wasn't. The young girl's real name is Gilda and her father was a real admiral. He died and she receives his pension.

How was it that the fellow had gotten my name? Ah, that I can't say, no way. I'm sorry. A professional secret.

As I told him, I explained everything about Gilda to him.

Every month, the clerk at the Navy Service office shouts from his window the name Admiral Jonas Tamanduá, who was her father. And who goes to pick up the money, swinging her hips, in the middle of that crowd of sailors, all of them drooling, but my sly friend Admiral. In other words, Gilda Tamanduá.

Do we work together? Look at our faces, of course, babe.

Then, that was it. The fellow called me and said, I'm bringing my friend Colonel. Then, it was my turn to ask for explanations. He told me that his name was Eduardo. He's got this nickname Colonel because his godfather was a powerful man from the backwoods. I don't know any more, one of those states y'know, one of those landowners in the Northeast that people call Colonel, y'know? I call him Eduardo, and he told me, you can call me what you want. He doesn't care. He's a pretty good guy, you'll see.

That one called Colonel, the King's friend, the Liberated Woman of the Penthouse reveals, didn't have anything left to him by his father. By the way, he doesn't even know who his father was. Maybe, his father was this big shot he called My Godfather Colonel Chico Guedes. It's possible, right? They say these fellows, wherever they're the boss, they knock up every woman, filling the world with bastards.

Great, I said, a bastard colonel is going for a fake admiral. You can come over tomorrow at 9 P.M. No problem. The building number is seventy. Not sixty. Seventy. Look buddy, 69 plus one. Got it now? What's the matter, can't you hear me? You just need to know the number of the building because at the penthouse there's only one apartment. Then, there'll be no mistake, I said. No there won't, honey, I said. I'll wait for you, bring your friend over. (The soccer player Colonel was something new. Most of the time we only know old colonels who are young girls' sugar daddies, right?)

Naked King

I'm naked and lonely.

Here I am sitting on this bench, the park is in front of me, huge and green, the river farther down, a bridge, people walking over it, taking a stroll. People are thinking about me at this moment, in this city, in China, Colombia, Senegal, wherever. Brazil, all over Europe, and in the United States, you don't even need to mention. Now all this talk about the faggot who came to save my life. I still don't know what kind of trap they're setting for me. This newspaper's headline exaggerates:

PLAN TO ASSASSINATE THE KING

Another newspaper insinuates that this could be a

publicity stunt to help promote my film *Pelé Plays Against Crime*. The press is terrible. These journalists want to screw me, they've already written that I consider myself more famous than Jesus Christ. Sometimes they misinterpret everything I say. Or they do it on purpose just to kick my balls. Once I said I *admired* Christ. He's the historical character I'm the most impressed by, I said. My role model. Then, just to shit my act, they published I had compared myself to Jesus. They're really a drag. They want to see me naked, defenseless. But I defend myself.

Here, there you go (the king shoots the bird at the landscape). You can't fool me, white folks.

Women of the Penthouse, According to Colonel

Yes, I remember very well. I'm not crazy. I'm not gonna talk to these newspaper men. They're all into destroying us, me and the King. Of course I can remember very well, how couldn't I? Brotha brought me along. Two sexy, nice chicks. That penthouse on General Osorio Square in Ipanema. A big fucking apartment. Everything first class. Stuffed with money, those ladies. And that's right, making a living as hookers. The one called Admiral had red hair, but not much hair on her pussy. I had never seen anything like that, something that'd make your mouth water. I bent down straight to that red haired pussy with my tongue, a first rate fuck. She had a good ass too and I checked that out 'cause I can't turn that down, no way, since I'm a good Brazilian, that big white asshole standing out on her beach tanned skin, oh, my God, so fucking good.

Oh yes, someone who knew the apartment owner — one of Brotha's contacts who knows it all — sold him the phone number for a hundred dollars. Some more information came with the number — both ladies' bank account numbers. That afternoon, we deposited the equivalent of 400 black market dollars into their account. Two hundred for each one. In other words, the date cost us 500 gringo bills. A big fucking wad of money. But the girls had class, the truth is they had a lot of class.

Liberated Woman of the Penthouse

My name is Laura. We gotta make a lot of dough. In our world he who has no money, who has no dough, is nobody, he's screwed up. He gets sick, and then what? He'll be in the hands of the Government or a Social Security hospital? Me, no way. It's not easy to keep such looks. Admiral knows it. She's chic, born with a silver spoon in her mouth, attended the best schools, and everything. She's a hooker like me. Her mother died and her father didn't want to get married again, so he could leave everything to her. The old man had brains, he guaranteed my friend's future. I bought this penthouse with my blood and sweat, folks, I know how much it cost me. Admiral was being taken for a ride by some assholes who only wanted her money. Then she found me, from a sucker she turned into a smart girl. That's the way, as my mother would say, who also made a living herself. What would become of the smart people if there were no suckers?

Men are dull, false and liars, we don't even know what to think of them. That one called Colonel? Sad, the hunk. He lay down on top of poor Admiral and fell asleep. Can you believe that? It wasn't easy for the poor woman to get out from underneath him. A strong guy, damned heavy, his whole weight on top of my friend. She managed to turn him sideways and kept looking at that animal, a real big horse. A huge chest, those hard and thick thighs, the stomach as flat as a piece of board, don't fall for him, I said when she breathlessly described that smartass's bulging body to me. Well, a real smartass, that didn't even work. But a beautiful body to watch, I confess. And I don't even care about men's looks. It was beautiful to see him walking in the house naked.

Nini? Ah, Nini, you're too dumb. And whoever is that dumb has to ask God to kill him and take him to the devil. Yeah. That's what I had to say to Nini. Her mistake was to believe us like a fool.

My Name is Gilda. You Can Call Me Admiral.

Admiral, she'll come over without a doubt. I've got some news I wanna tell you personally.

I went there and Laura immediately showed me our joint account's balance, which, of course, made me very, very happy.

Then Laura called Nivaldo, our Nini Wonder, for him to doll us up, do our nails, toes, hair and all that jazz. Nini is great, but a bit soft in the head. Isn't that proven now? A bit? Completely mad. Well, when she knew who was coming that night she almost had a fit. She was madly in love, she told us, with Pelé. How could we have guessed it? If you wish, Laura said, we can ask him for an autograph for you. Then the faggot almost went totally crazy. She had a mound of the fellow's pictures, cut out of magazines. She knew everything about his career, the smart girl. She watched every game, but only on TV. She was afraid of going to the stadiums because they said soccer is a man's thing, for machos, and the faggots, you see, are chased away. Nini went to Maracanã Stadium once, and the poor thing was unlucky enough to watch the game among the losing team's fans. Then, a freak shouted pointing at her, it was this big fag who brought bad luck to our team. He started, out of the blue, slapping the poor devil's face. Nini ran away, she was chased, totally ashamed. She never dared to go back, poor thing, to face any other stadium like Maracanã. She was crazy for soccer and Pelé. Completely mad.

When Laura, after being mysterious, decided to reveal her guest's name, Nini had a fit. I brought her a glass of water and sugar to calm her down, drink it, babe, and cut it out. Fortunately she was about to finish her work when she found out about it, just a few retouches on the nails and that I could do for my friend and myself. Nini could go to hell. We didn't need her any more. She could beat it.

A few days later, we made up that joke. Laura called the simpleton and told her she had heard of a plan to assassinate Pelé. A very complicated thing. Laura mixed up the Mafia with a group of South American subversives plus a secret sect of American racists. To sum up, a big mess. They were going to kill the guy, Laura said, because he had refused to make a public appeal for the release of a few Brazilian political prisoners, and also because he had married a white woman and the blacks in the U.S. were furious at him. I didn't understand very well what Laura was setting up, but I confirmed everything she'd said and I tried to add fuel to the fire, backed up by a cop friend who was also having fun with the trick on crazy Nini. So we set up the day, time and place where the so-called fella, the murderer, was going to pull out his gun and shoot Pelé. Then, Nini went completely crazy and disappeared.

Admiral takes a look at the picture in the paper, showing Pelé being kissed by The Smile Child From the West Coast, and says, Poor Nini, but she'll be OK, right? Big titted faggot. But that's it. We only intended to play a little trick on her. Well, everything happens in that country, right?

Stains in the Night

On the eve of the assassination attempt Nini saw on TV, in the rundown Hall Hotel in the alley in Brooklyn, the trophy awards ceremony. On the *Warner Bros.* fifteenth floor, midtown Manhattan, impeccable in his Pierre Cardin suit, Pelé hands a golden soccer trophy to the winner of The Smile Child From the West Coast contest, a freckled blond kid named Donald Vitasay.

On the following morning, at the time and place revealed by her friends, Nini waits for her idol at the exit after a game between the Cosmos and the Minnesota Kings. Almost dead frozen by New York's winter. Wrapped in a brown fur coat. A lot of men wear raincoats, overcoats. Easy to hide a gun. To take the trip, Nini sold her VW bug, paid the Government a deposit of 22 thousand *cruzeiros* to be able to leave the country, and didn't complain about anything. She left and there she was, in the cold, in the heart of that violent city. And when the soccer star, surrounded by friends, was leaving the stadium, Nini soon saw a suspicious man get close. Then, she ran toward Pelé. She covered his body, opening her arms like a cross, at the exact moment the murderer shot his gun.

Two shots in the chest and one in the face, someone said, but he'll be OK. Nivaldo feels pain, and thinks, thankful, above all, that it's good to be alive. (When we're all dead, will there be a thorough explanation?)

Afterwards, in the hospital, asked by a journalist, if he repented his madness, Nini Wonder said no, had I more lives, I would sacrifice all of them for him.

On his bedroom TV, the end of an old movie, *The King in New York*, shows the warning that this is a work of fiction and all events and characters depicted are fictitious, any resemblance to anyone living or dead is merely coincidental, and next, in big letters and covering the whole screen, the words

The End

WOMAN IN THE GAME

1

● Mané got that bird over there as a present after the game against the Argentines. Mané dribbled three and broke a tie, giving Brazil the victory. It's a very good singing *curio.* (In this interview singer Elsa Soares reveals that she's writing a book about her life with Manuel Francisco dos Santos, the soccer star Mané Garrincha).

2

○ Honey, that's the gold medal that Marcos captured after blocking a penalty shot, guaranteeing a win for Brazil in an important match against Argentina. (In our series of interviews with the wives of the most renowned soccer players of all times we're listening to poetess Ana Amélia, married to goalkeeper Marcos de Mendonça, one of the first idols of Brazilian soccer.)

● Wait a sec, Elsinha. Gotta test this piece of junk to see if its really recording. Sometimes, if you fool around, when you try to get it on paper there's nothing. I swear it's already happened to me.

○ Attention, recording. When did that happen, Ana Amélia?

● Why Mané (the book's gonna be called *My Life with Mané*) if everybody knows him as Garrincha? Elsa rolls her eyes before answering.

○ A long, long time ago, honey. (Ana's look seems to be far away, in the past).

Samba and Soccer

● Because Garrincha belongs to everybody, right, darling? And Mané here belongs only to the Chocolate Goddess. I also call 'im Baby. Because he's got those crooked legs, right?

Sonnet and Soccer

○ He got that medal and I wrote him a few verses. A sonnet.

● Along with her memoirs the singer/songwriter is going to release the samba *A Story to Provoke You,* written with Gérson Alves.

○ Do you like it? Do you really want me to? Will I remember everything right? (Pause. Ana Amélia recites part of the poem written a half century ago.)

● Can you sing a snatch of the song for us, Elsa?

○ *Like a Greek warrior after a victory,/ who brought his beloved lady the laurel/ You came to bring me this gold medal/ the symbol of brilliance that crowns your glory.*

● *This love of ours/ nothing can be done about it/ I learned to love your faults. This themesong of ours/ is still gonna turn out to be one more popular samba.*

○ That is so old. One of my first attempts to be a poetess, honey.

● That's right. I've always been the black lady of Samba. I've never denied being a samba singer, while the other singers call themselves interpreters. Ah, how I met Mané? Yeah, I'll tell ya.

○ They were very successful attempts. The poetess married her Greek warrior and published eight books which received a good response from the critics. Ana Amélia sketches her past and reminisces about how she met Marcos de Mendonça.

Love Enters the Field

● I was invited to sing to the players after one of the Brazilian National Team's training sessions. Then I met Mané. He's such a fool. He confessed to me that he's even got a son with a Swedish woman. He made time for that during the 1958 World Cup which sanctified Brazilian soccer. But that was before the hero met this little lady here. Now I watch him very closely.

Love Enters the Field

○ I was invited to watch a game at the America's stadium. Ah, how happy I was on that afternoon (the year was 1913) coming back home. While the match was on, I made friends with a few nice girls who were sitting nearby, in the stands.

● He kissed me the day we met. I have a newspaper clipping I want to show ya. Look how cool it is. The reporter talks about the show I was going to give and asks the players what they think 'bout it.

Look who's the only one to say
somethin'. Mané, of course. Elsa
sings well and she's cute. Y'see?
The bum already had an eye on the
doll here. And I, the innocent girly
girl, was very quiet in a corner.
That's just for you t' see.

○ She talks with pauses and at
times so softly that it takes an
added effort to hear her sentences
completely. Ana Amélia speaks
as if she is reexperiencing
everything she reminisces.

● Honey, what a guy. But what
was I saying? Ah, yes. I went to
give the show for the players who
were gathered in Friburgo. Yes, the
1962 World Cup. In Chile. After
his kiss, I felt like getting to know
Mané better.

○ It so happened that those
young girls were the goalie's
cousins. At half time Marcos
came to chat with them.

● Asked if she knows Garrincha's
wife, if Dona Nair has ever looked
for her, the singer says: Don't

know'er. (After a pause, as if she refused to talk, Elsa goes on.) But everybody knows that I was not the second in Mané's life. And don't go calling me *the other woman*. Knock on wood. I'm not the kind of woman you call a home breaker. He had lotsa others, in Brazil and abroad, before me. Baby doesn't fool around. He's real hot.

O Then, we were introduced. I fell in love with Marcos at that very moment. And I think he likewise.

● Our wedding was in '65, the papers were issued in the Bolivian Embassy. I showed up wearing sports pants, and after that, we had coffee. Our duo had already been going on for four years, with everything you can think of. At this point in the championship, so to speak, we could not hide our game any more.

O Good ol' times were those days of pure amateurism when the players came over to speak with the female supporters during the match intervals in the soccer stadium. (Reporter's comment interspersed with the interviewee's statements which the editor keeps.)

● Everything?

○ Pregnant by emotion, that's what the poetess reveals she felt like. And soon these first verses were born, dedicated to her hero: *It was under the blue sun, in golden May/ one day that I met you. Handsome like Apollo,/ and my love was born, in luminous ray,/ like the seed crushing the wet soil.*

● I was already pregnant by Mané, darling.

○ Ah, you said I was Parnassian-like in love? Parnassian-like, deeply in love.

● Only to make sure. That's what I thought.

○ When they got married, the goalkeeper became a very

dedicated businessman. (The editor crossed out the words *very dedicated,* and the sentence went: After their wedding, Marcos de Mendonça efficiently undertook the business affairs, etc.)

● One more voice. Sara smiles. A little girl with crooked legs.

○ In our family, there were no male heirs, honey. Then Marcos was director of the Good Hope Steel Mill.

● There are two things Baby wants very badly. A son (he's got only daughters) and to go back to soccer. As a player or a coach. Baby still has a whole world of things to offer the fans.

○ Nothing more natural (comment by the article's editor) than Ana Amélia to see in her beloved goalie a *doublé* of a university student, a cultured fellow, an expert on history, the very incarnation of the Greek ideal of intellectual-athlete. They lived in the soccer lace-cuffed era.

An elitist sport practiced only by the top employees of the British companies that were established here and a few well-to-do Brazilians who bought the precious equipment in Europe for the so-called *noble Briton sport.*

Mané's Era

● When Mané was at his best, he by himself guaranteed a complete sell-out.

Marcos's Era

○ In the album (look, honey), the description of the Fluminense stands by Peregrino Junior, a promising social columnist in 1919: a pinky dazzling sight. He compares the female supporters (here, that's me) to a bouquet of flowers.

● In her memoirs, Elsa denounces doping in Brazilian soccer. Those little injections to his knees pushed Mané to play in bad physical condition and destroyed his health. Don't you see, Mané was worth half the Botafogo team? If he didn't play, only half of the total tickets were sold.

○ In Marcos' time, young men paid to play. The club only provided them with the ball and the club facilities. All of the sports equipment had to be bought by the athlete. Marcos paid Fluminense five thousand *réis* a month. Today, I know almost two hundred thousand people go to Maracanã to see a big game, isn't it true? In that time, honey, if there was a audience of two thousand people to see a match it was an enormous success.

● His disappointments run deep. And he's got a lot of them. But Mané doesn't like to talk about 'em. It's me who lets the cat outta the bag. I can't stand all the dirt they threw and still throw at him.

○ Regatta. The most popular sport in Rio at that time was regatta, which took place in the pleasant waters of Guanabara Bay.

● When Mané's father, who was the watchman at the fabrics factory in Pau Grande, died, a few big shots said that they would make a point of attending the burial. They called that whole thing a last homage to our idol's father. And Mané believed it.

○ Brazilian soccer (a comment inserted in the article by the sports editor) was far from being grand, this only happened after it touched the lowest social class from which almost every soccer star came, giving Brazilian soccer its worldwide reputation.

● The singer lights up a cigarette and changes her position on the sofa before she continues to speak.

○ With soccer's growing popularity, it was necessary that the players were the best and the teams were continuously training. The athletes had to dedicate themselves entirely. It was no longer a hobby as it had been for the young fellows in Marcos' generation. The clubs started to pay their athletes a salary so that they could dedicate themselves to soccer 24 hours a day. By the beginning of the 20s, the end of amateurism was already clear. Real professional soccer actually began much later, I know, but what we called brown amateurism started to pick up, something similar to what would happen later to basketball and tennis in Brazil. Anyway, that was an important step. People from lower classes started devoting themselves to soccer. The audience grew in an extraordinary way. We've already commented on that, haven't we? The clubs' income grew and they, consequently, could offer their athletes a little more. Today, Marcos always says, if the good players know how to get organized, they can become very rich men.

● And Garrincha continued to believe. The big shots are going to show up. . .

○ Marcos was always praised by the sports journalists, and, often he was applauded by his opponents. During a game in England once, the Corinthians' athletes even applauded his defenses. That gesture gives you an idea of the prestige, consideration and respect they had towards him. But those were very romantic times, weren't they?

● Mané said: Let's wait, folks, 'cause the big shots are coming for sure. The big shots were the directors of the clubs. Those guys, that riffraff. The garbage truck driver says he can't wait no more. The cemetery closes at five. They're waiting for us because it's you, your dad. But now we gotta decide. What a shame. A degradation for the world's champion, the People's Joy, the player who the King of Sweden made a point of greeting, of shaking hands with at the stadium after the 1958 World Cup final. Mané finally made up his mind. Yeah, good people, it seems that the big shots couldn't find the way up here this time.

Ah, believe me, a few other times, a lot of times, they found the way to Pau Grande all right and went there, to that backwater, to speak with him patiently, see

Mané's little birds, pamper him and
to take advantage of him in the
signing of his contract with a club.
A pack of cuckolds.

It was a very sad day for Baby.
The end of a dream. The loss of his
prestige. Discredited before the
factory workers, his friends.

A Lot in Common

O Yes, we have a lot of
affinities, without a doubt. We
both write. I write those verses
which you already know, and
Marcos, you know, Marcos is a
historian. In my opinion he is the
only person who's able to write
about certain historical areas of
the Brazilian economy. In
particular, metallurgy.

A Lot in Common

● A lot in common? Yes, we're
really similar. We both were factory
workers. We have a difficult past
full of disappointments,
humiliations. These things draw
people together all right. Now we
have our love, which is what
matters the most.

○ Our love continues. And I can't forget that strong impression the first time I laid eyes on him in white jersey and shorts, the soccer shoes tied up with white laces. And the famous dark purple ribbon which Marcos used to wear around his waist, taken out of the hat I wore to the stadium that day.

● It's all written in the book. I'm a five-foot black woman, but at times I jump up to six feet. When I get my heart filled up with love. Like right now.

○ Yes, the Purple Ribbon was undoubtedly a great idol of our sport. Marcos was only 16 when, in 1911, the newspapers in Rio started to give more space to soccer, by expert journalists excited by his performances.

● I don't like to talk about racial discrimination, don't like to sound like an American black. But the problem exists, yes, it really does. I've felt it right in my face many times.

O Daughter of the engineer José Joaquim de Queirós, pioneer in metallurgy, Ana Amélia in her own way contributed to the promotion and popularization of soccer. Including acting as a coach.

● Her first husband — white, *Italianized* (as she describes him) — used to compare their skin color and said that he was superior. (He beat her.) At the San Raphael hotel, in São Paulo, Elsa and Garrincha were not admitted as guests because they were not married, while white couples were not asked for their marriage certificates at the reception desk. In the clubs, including those where she sang and Garrincha played, they were not allowed to attend the parties. Let your mouths hang open, even at Flamengo, which is said to belong to the masses, Elsa explains angrily.

O It's true that you taught the bosses's game to their workers. (Ana Amélia smiles reminiscing about the past.)

● Let it be, darling. The important

thing is that now we're happy. The
thing is to go on with the game.

○ Sure, and after young people
started to play, I guided them, I
gave them technical advice.

● Born to a washerwoman and a
factory worker, Elsa made up for
her poor childhood by holding onto
the belief that things would change
some day.

○ At a time when kicking the
ball up in the air was what thrilled
the public (and there were players
who became famous for their
ability to kick the ball higher than
any other), with her revolutionary
tactical vision, Ana Amélia
discovered that that was a big
mistake. The important thing is
to send the ball forward. Soccer
is not played in the air. It's on
ground level and forward.

● My father was a factory worker.
Didn't go to school, but he was a
very cool man. He knew how t' use
his mind. He made a point of
sending me to school. At only four,

the doll here could already read. At seven I finished primary school. As soon as I could, I left the slum, coming down the hill, I became a samba singer when that name was pejorative, a synonym for the slum, gang of blacks, niggers. Only after I recorded my first album (you see how powerful an album is), those who looked askance at me — she turned up her nose — started to listen to me, she says smiling.

O The article's editor got exited about Ana Amélia's knowledge of soccer. Fantastic. This woman has an incredible intuition. Really, almost the same advice Coach João Saldanha repeated to Pelé, Gerson and Co., during training for the World Cup in Mexico.

In 1970, Saldanha said: It's no use trying to lob inside the penalty area. Let's beat the gringos with the ball rolling on the ground.

Beginnings: A Trip

● It was a prize I won on Ary Barroso's singing contest program that allowed me to take a taxi for the first time. Back then I still lived in the slum. But the host, can you believe, wanted me to send the prize money to the poor. But Mr. Barroso, I said to him, it happens that this black girl here in front of you is also poor. That was a laugh. I said that on the mike and the man almost swallowed the little harmonica that he used for honking the young singers. Then, I took my first taxi, which cost me ten *cruzeiros*. That was how, mounted on wheels, I got to the slum that day. Total glory.

Beginnings: A Trip

O If you wanted perfect printing, you had to have your book printed abroad, in Europe. That was in 1911. Ana Amélia published her first book in Paris: *Expectations*. Critic João do Rio's opinion: Either these verses are not by this child or this child is a tropical Shelley. In her baggage back to Brazil, the 15-year-old girl brought from Europe under her arm not only a book (her book) but also a few soccer balls.

● Elsa, after a long puff, looks serious: But don't we have to talk about Mané?

○ Haven't we already talked about that? At that time, good sports equipment had to be purchased in Europe.

● Both. About you and him.

○ Interest in soccer is a constant in Ana Amélia's life. It got bigger, naturally, after meeting Marcos. But it is from a long way back, before their meeting. When she turned 12, she had already asked her parents for a birthday present, a ball and thick-soled boots. Today she calls herself a woman who defends soccer-finesse, but reveals that, during the game's battle, she even practiced rugged soccer. And with stamina that made the most vigorous backs jealous.

● Elsa tells how she was a housekeeper. Concerning that time, she had a few personal and juicy observations. She suggests, for example, that some housewives should try what she called a maid's transplant. And explains, back then when she worked in those ladies' houses, her bosses kept obstinately pinching her, always more interested in going to bed with her than with their own wives.

O With a boot kick, Ana Amélia caused her sister Jujuca (the future wife of the president of the Brazilian Academy of Letters, Austregésilo de Athayde), who was very delicate, to lay unconscious on the ground.

Ninth Floor: Cuttings

● Is the book just about your life with Garrincha or do you also talk about other love affairs?

Ninth Floor: Insertions

O Since you like to mess around with the chest of souvenirs, honey, in there there's an often cited poem, because the experts say that it truthfully, introduced the soccer theme into Brazilian poetry. It's called *The Jump* and, you can imagine, I was inspired by watching Marcos who seemed to have wings. Really, Marcos seemed to be flying in order to defend a forward's kick. It's sonnet which ends like this : *Like a god who descends from Olympus, graceful and cheerful,/ you touched the soil, at last, glorious, ardent, and fearless,/ and your beauty is worthy of the Greek canon.*

● Everybody knows that Mané was not the first man in my life. I got married when I was twelve, and soon, I was pregnant. Yes, I am also talking about the others. Why deny those things? No use embellishing the game. And most of them just wanted to exploit me. My life hasn't been that easy. My past has not been a piece of cake. Real difficult.

○ That's good, honey, the article's editor says. A real top notch job.

● Ah, that thing about inspiration? (The question was

meant to reveal something about her method of writing her memoirs.) A good screw with Mané, my angel, and I feel inspired, Elsa says maliciously.

That's good, the article's editor says to the reporter. But the boss up there (he points indicating the ninth floor of the newspaper building) may not O.K. that thing about racial discrimination — you know, Nascentes has written a book in order to support his thesis of Brazilian racial democracy — and, of course, we need to change certain words by Elsa Soares.

○ No cutting this time? On the contrary, honey. There will even be an insertion suggested by the ninth floor. (The young reporter found out that the director-president of *The Nation's Journal* was also a historian and, therefore, Marcos' colleague.) Put that ending over there in your report, my angel. Nascentes Borges wrote it himself. Then end with Ana Amélia's part, of course.

● The singer finally revealed that she enjoys writing in bed (picture

of Elsa laying in bed with her feet
on Garrincha's legs) and every time
she has the soccer star beside her,
she feels inspired.

○ That's why, when Marcos de
Mendonça goes to the tea
meetings at the Brazilian National
Historical Institute, he leaves his
colleagues bewildered by saying
I come to meet with you every
week, but I am really going to be
remembered as a soccer player.

Nobody's going to forget the
famous Purple Ribbon, he says in
a good-humored way.

(DOUBLE CURTAIN)

BYE, BYE SOCCER

Thin shins, 36, five and a half feet tall, 156 pounds. A Brazilian with an incredible ability with the ball. Me, Anselmo, the one people talk about. The press used to praise me like this a long time ago: The incredibly skilled Anselmo. My technique. My father, my mother. That wife, my son. My pal and friend Nelsão. From cheers to jeers. Everything happened so fast. Want one more sip? Can't go on without a *cachaça*. Glub, glub, glub, from the bottle. It's damn cold. My head's spinning, spinning. Good ol' times when I scored goals, lots of them. The goddamned goals (my repertoire: volleying sideways, scissors, and heel kicks) are never enough. That cheap, son-of-a-gun referee. That shitty sports commentator said that I was running to nowhere. I wasn't getting to the net, to the explosion, to the goal. They wanted goals, goals, goals. One more. Always one more. They asked me to explode. I'm not a bomb, damn it, what was that shit all about?

My poor old buddy, he's really in bad shape. Just yesterday, I went to visit him. Hi Anselmo, how's it goin'? And I ended up thinking that he didn't recognize me. He's been in the hospital for a week. Drugged by so much medicine, it was sad to see that still young man disfigured by so many nervous tics. Where's the kid famous for his deadly dribbling, who dummied the defense so easily, who never got tired of running to the touchline? And all that happening just four, five years ago, just like yesterday.

After all, I could never face those special diets. That thing about doing the so-called musculation workout when you're still growing didn't get me, this kid here didn't go for that, oh, no. But also I never suffered a very bad bruise. Ah, to avoid that, sir, is an art I'd learned when I was a street kid. I don't have a great build, I know, or broad shoulders, I know, because I was born and raised a poor kid, malnourished. Then I always had to use my ability, my technique, yes, it's true I always avoided charging, but the real game is won by kicking, intelligence and the feint.

Anselmo, the little frail black kid, running after the ball made out of socks in squares in Mendes, Rio de Janeiro, Brazil. Running away from the stronger boys' blows and from his watchful father's eyes, a railroad worker, who wanted him to graduate one day. A doctor or a lawyer or an engineer. A doctor. Studying was not his thing at the General Flavio Jaguaribe Savary Public School. He was much more familiar with the ball (which rolled freely) than with books. The gang gathered in the little square, and we played our little soccer game.

In the good old days, he was really happy, like a kid, playing tricks on everybody, he made a dummy with his clothes and put it in his bed at a hotel where the team was staying, fooling the coach's watchful eye. He cheated Coach Verissimo, and ran away, sometimes for a date with a girl whose heart he'd won, Anselmo was hot, or simply to be with a group of friends sipping drinks somewhere, enjoying himself at a bar, and he would do those things on the eve of an important game. Take it easy, my friend, I told him endlessly. But when the game was on, it was he who made the decisions, it was from his feet that the most perfect passes started, let alone the goals, it was he who reversed the games, it was he who played every position, who disputed every ball, he who even played without a ball just to cleverly fool his marker. A great soccer star, but I was always concerned about him during the half-time break, drinking a cuba-libre out of a little Coca-Cola bottle. I'm foolin' everybody, his eyes seemed to be saying to me. I looked at him and he looked at me showing that he knew that I knew that it was not a soft-drink and that he was not foolin' anybody, no not the crazy Anselmo, but himself.

My father got pissed off at me, the eldest, with eight more children to care for in the house, and very little dough, almost not enough for beans and *manioc* flour and it was me who wanted to become a soccer player. He made the decision that I finish high school, and more courses. I was sent to Campos and enrolled in an accounting course, it didn't take long for me to meet Major Gabeira. A very respected man in town, a retired police major, the president of the Sugar Cane Planter's Cooperative. I played soccer a lot on his ranch. You're good, kid, you've got a future. He brought me to Rio. Room, board and a little cash by the end of the month. I tried to continue with the accounting, but after attending two or three classes I quit. I learned Rio's suburban loafing. I already had the technique, and when I debuted for Flamengo I showed 'em my style. I went up the career ladder fast, the following year I was a pro at 19. Soon, one of Rio's champion goal scorers, a coveted forward, ready for the Brazilian National Team. The first bad sign was when they started to say that Anselmo complained too much in every game. It happens that each player has his own way. I, for example, am a grouser, since I was a boy I'd admired Almir and Silva, I liked their way of grousing on the field.

Boos, curses, critiques, disgusting chants from the stands. In the beginning they kept shouting my name, demanding the big shots nominate me for the National Team, then, all of a sudden, demanding they sell my contract to that team of flat-headed players from Paiuí. He was branded, the crowds didn't accept his attitude any more. Sometimes a player may be right. It's only on the field that you can say something. The mess was made, I saw that Anselmo had touched the ball with his hand, but it did no good and when he was about to fall their goalkeeper came and kicked my friend who'd already lost the ball. The referee pretended he hadn't seen anything, and that's when I think my friend lost his temper, they never agree with a player who complains on these occasions. Off the field we can't say anything. I'm speaking about the game when I was not on the field, I'd already hung up my soccer shoes for good, so to speak.

There's no other explanation, everything was thought over to damage you, my friend. I'm a goal scorer, I'm a grouser. As I said many times at Gávea, Almir and Silva were the ones I admired most, renowned grousers, my biggest models. I was born right there at the Miguel Couto hospital in front of Flamengo Stadium. My mother had come to visit one of her sisters, Aunt Irene, who washed clothes for those ladies and she lived up there in the Rochinha slum. At that time, the Atlantida Studios comedies were a tremendous success. My mother was crazy about the young leading actor of all those movies, someone called Anselmo Dinarte, or Duarte, or something like that,

and my father had the hots for that Adelaide something, a
foreign name, a lady with a big ass who played the
accordion. To my mother, that Anselmo from the movies
was the most handsome man ever and my father, to take
revenge on mother, screwed the young actress-musician
Adelaide in his dreams almost every night for ten, fifteen
years on end. I was seven or eight years old, and kept
listening to him speak to a few of his friends that came
over for a beer, a *cachaça* or for an aimless chat, about the
filthy things he did with Adelaide. My poor Mom also
heard him. I think he wanted her to hear him really. My old
mother would leave the living-room crying, if it's a girl
her name will be Adelaide, my father said when I was
about to be born, but his prediction flopped, it was not a
girl. That was me, I was in a hurry, an eight-month
pregnancy, Mom was visiting Aunt Irene and was only
expecting me the following month, a month later. And
here I was to make my father angry, little Anselmo at
home. Mom told me all that when I was already a grown-
up, it was sheer luck, my father thought I was spitting in
his face and didn't care about my name. Didn't give a
damn.

It's something that gets you really down, man, to play
and know that every time you touch the ball, you're gonna
get booed or even cursed. Calm down, chum, take it easy,
I said to Anselmo, but I saw he could only stand it all
thanks to drinking his *cachaça* and he was gonna screw it,
that was clear. He'd been drinking since he was ten, when
his father gave him his first sip, and his father died of
cirrhosis, poor Valdomiro, the dream of winning Adelaide
Chiozzo's heart, the other day I saw one of her old movies
on TV and I remembered how bad he felt for her and the
dream of his son becoming a doctor, all those dreams, right
Valdomiro? His prediction flopped. Anselmo was the eldest,

then came a host of eight boys with no girl to name after the Accordion Queen. In that game Anselmo was benched and booed. He was learning his lesson the hard way. A player is only wanted when he's at the top, doing well, scoring a lot of goals. Then the player gets more confident and is more in control of himself on the field. Anselmo lost his head. Then he told me the referees were on his back all the time. That's possible. In my case, it was different, people don't ask too much from a defense player. It is also true that a defense player will hardly become an idol, though. Anyway, my build was good enough to get by, I could be a discreet and esteemed player. But if the guy is a forward, a goal scorer that doesn't score goals, then he's fucked up, he's really sacrificed, and begins to feel lonely, a victim of injustice, forgotten, abused. That's what happened and Anselmo was drinking as usual, cursing the referees and on top of that he was jealous of his wife who couldn't stand it any longer. He was beating her. All that because he was not scoring goals. And I saw, when I went to look for my pal in the locker room, that nobody said a single hello to him, not even hi. We left and walked past about thirty reporters and photographers, and nobody paid attention to him, and I knew that hurt him, and he once had been applauded and flattered by those same people. He kept cursing the referees and trying to drag me to a bar.

That son-of-a-bitch referee, damn it, before the beginning of the game, he came to me and said, I'm gonna send you outta the game, you snot, he said it softly so I was the only one to hear him, that was meant to irritate me, so when I started to play I was already nervous. The pig had surely been bribed to harass me for no reason, I spat and said nothing. Then he went to speak to the two team captains, and during the first dangerous rushdown in the opponent's goal area, he sent me out, the scumbag. I was running in their goal area and I really touched the ball, it didn't help, I lost my balance, I fell, and their disgusting goalie came and fouled me. I'd already lost the ball, the guy kicked me and the son-of-a-bitch referee pretended he didn't see anything, that crook. I went to talk to him, am I obliged to be beaten and keep quiet and you didn't even whistle? I didn't insult him, no it's he who asked me to shut up, but I kept talking because I couldn't believe what had happened. Then, he always speaking softly, called me a monkey and said he was going to beat me up, but said all that in a very calm way as if he wasn't putting me down at all. I already knew the son-of-a-bitch was going to throw me out of the game anyway. Cuckold faggot. I shoulda beaten the shit outta him right there, but I didn't do it, chum, I still had control over myself, don't know how, and he did what he threatened he was going to do, that was it, that was what he wanted to do at first, to kick me out of the game. To the showers. Shitty referee.

Everybody got to know about it because even the police were in on the story. My buddy beat his wife, not once or twice, but many times. She told me. I can't stand this hell any more, and said that Anselmo got home drunk and wanted to sleep with her, his breath smelling of the *cachaça* she couldn't stand. Then, she said, I refused it and that's when he said I was going out with another man. Yesterday was like that, I said no to him, and I swore I had nobody, but I wasn't going to continue behaving like the angel I have been, then he grabbed me, threw me in bed and clutched my throat as if he were going to kill me. She managed to get rid of him and went to file a complaint with the police, then, I asked 'em to drop the charges in spite of being completely right, and she said, I swear, I was really into it, I only wanted to teach'im a lesson. Sure. I'll drop the charges, let's go there, but she still said, I don't want him any more. At least, she said, we need to give ourselves some time apart, he's gotta go away from me, just send me money to support our son, I'll get by. That was a little before Anselmo went to the North, and then, for a long time, I didn't know how he was doing and how his problem with his wife was. Not long ago she showed up and told me she was raising the kid all by herself. Better this way, isn't it? He couldn't conform, he telephoned and called me names. I could tell he was drunk on the phone, if you go on like that you'll kill yourself and I don't want it to happen in my bed, that's why for me his homecoming was no good. Lately, it was too unbearable for her, he wouldn't let go of his glass, you know, from early morning until late at night he held a glass or didn't even use a glass, he'd drink outta the bottle. He only drank, from morning to night, a man who was good for nothing. I know he won't change, he's finished. You said he could recover, but he's really in bad shape, rotten, he bad-mouthed everything specially the teams he's not playing for. I think he's gotten worse once and for all.

When you find yourself alone among the backs, most of the time there's nobody to come and carry the ball to the other side. Everybody's back there, and there's no way. I can't work miracles all by myself, this team of flat-heads. That's tough. Our mid-fielders don't move forward enough and what happens? You get the ball, have to spin around and still break their defensive wall. That's no good, it's impossible to get something outta this. On this shitty team, that's what happens: the one who gets the ball has to get rid of it as soon as possible, passing it to the side or if it's time to shoot to goal, he tried to pass to a teammate and he's the one who's gotta do something about it, who'll be booed by the crowds if he missed the goal. The fans are a drag. There's something else. This field is in terrible shape

and forces the team to shoot the ball up in the air, that's
what the coach demands, ball to the air, and now he's got
a good argument backing his tactics, because a bad joke
happened last week, a player broke his foot stepping into
one of the holes on this field. Field my ass, hardly any
grass because there's much more sand here instead. Shit.
Then, I talked to Coach Inocencio, that's what's wrong,
sir, these midfielders are playing tight, I find myself alone
in the front without any support. But the crowds are not
interested in discussing such problems, he answered, the
crowds pay tickets to see goals, to celebrate victories,
Anselmo. When that's not possible they ask for our heads.

Anselmo's last day at Gávea was damn sad. I went
there to watch training. I'd hung up my soccer shoes a
couple of years earlier and had opened my own little sports
equipment store, minding my own life. I still used my feet
all right, not on the field, but on a paved avenue, parading
in green-and-pink for Mangueira, my Samba School, in
Carnival. I have been faithful to Mangueira since I was a
boy and in love with Samba Schools from the time they
really belonged to the people, before they turned into this
rowdy show for rich, jerky gringos to enjoy themselves.
But Mangueira will always be Mangueira, my old beloved
Mangueira, and every year I parade in the students' group,
which, by the way, has no students. But going back to
Anselmo. I went there and saw my old friend in the middle
of a few players in a circle. After warming up, they started
kicking and passing the ball in a one on one style and
kicking to goal. Then I heard one fan shouting, where's
that flighty Anselmo? And another answered he's the fool
still in the middle of the circle as usual. Had Anselmo also
heard that? I hope not, I thought to myself at once. On the
first ball he missed, someone whistled. On the second,
someone booed. On the goal he didn't score because he

tried to head the ball he'd received from a perfect corner kick, sending the ball outta the field, everybody booed him, and that he certainly heard. For a moment, he stopped on the field, and motionless, he scrutinized every bleacher, trying to spot the reason for that. Goals. They demanded he score goals. When his contract was offered for trade I thought a change of air would do him some good. The drinking problem had grown plus the arguments growing more and more violent, the fights, that whole mess, the police involved. Deep shit.

I know I'm not a player for charging. I've got my style. Beautiful game, that's what everybody always tells me, a classic style, very technical, I was always praised like that. They say that soccer now is physical strength, so let's call those guys from the regatta to the fields. There are a few of them so strong that they look like horses. Let's free them in the fields and see if it works out with those heavy guys playing soccer. There was this game I tried to go for every dribble, I tried to fight for every ball, I tried to quit my own style of playing, I left the field with my shirt all blood-stained and our team lost. Fuck.

He asked me, what's going on? You're missing goals, chum, I said. And when that happens it's really tough. The fans start to demand that the reserves go in. I told him, the fans demand goals and if there are no goals, they want to change that forward who's on the field, their rage and dissatisfaction falls on him. That's really tough, Anselmo said.

Goals, everybody missed them. Even the greatest goal scorers of Brazil play three, four games without scoring a single little goal. But from me, they demand goals in every game, in every training, they want me to score those goddamned goals by force. And now they accuse me of only jumpin'. Well, that's part of what they say when they don't have anything to say, pal, they are little groups of people that are into crucifying me like Christ, into destroying me, and I don't even know why, my game is like that, it has always been, I am a technical player, I was never into charging in a game. I am not a wrestler, damn it, I am a soccer player, fuck, and I want to be fucking respected. Oh, fuck.

On yesterday's visit, at times he seemed to be delirious during our conversation. I may not get to the touchline ninety times like in the past, he said, in a hoarse and faded voice, but I am almost thirty, chum, and my dribbling is still the same. I will turn thirty, I will. Yesterday there was a lot of lightning in the sky here, he said almost without a stop, and I was scared and so was my little bird, Filó. When I saw Anselmo back from Piauí, I was terrified. I went to see Doctor Santos who was the physician for the club when I was a player and we brought Anselmo to this clinic and checked him into the emergency room. My buddy's most faithful friend now was that little bird. The bird belonged to a friendly nurse who took care of both of them. I was frightened by my friend's state, his eyes were bulging out of his head, I'm here, I'm back, he said. Poor Anselmo, he was back without cheers, without money, without his wife, she was everything I cared about, chum. Have you seen my son, is he already talking and walking? I beat her up because she was betraying me, soccer also betrayed me. The two things I loved the most in life, my wife and soccer. Both were taken from me by other men, old friend. The health clinic is an old mansion, high ceilings, with a beautiful garden all around, peaceful. Not long ago, Doctor Santos telephoned with alarming news. He ran away, Santos said to me, nobody knows where to find him.

I'm worried, Doctor Santos said, because one more sip and he can end up going insane for good, his brain is too affected, if he touches alcohol it could be the end.

He had his coat on because he felt cold, it also helped him hide the bottle of *cachaça* which he had traded for his little bird Filó at the bar. The stadium was empty, what a world that Maracanã. Everything was silent now, where's the general admission crowd shouting his name? I was still a boy, 19 or something. I am not as irresponsible as they say. I'm a serious pro. I am not here for fun, no, I worked hard to make my name famous. When I got here from the countryside, a poor kid, I remember pretty well, the tall buildings gave me the chills, I avoided walking near them, the cars on the streets seemed to be crazy things, I trembled. The neon signs flashed, flashed, the store windows showed all those beautiful things, fine shirts, chrome polished shoes, I was going to be able to buy all of that, and a big car, and was going to win every woman's heart in the world. I trembled with excitement. A crazy city, women at my feet, most of them hookers, ready for anything. Where are those shouting fans, the crowds, their flags, their fireworks? When I sent that ball into the net like a cannon and we won the final game against Vasco, the sea of people sang the *Farewell Waltz*. Farewell, it's time to go. How did it really go? They sang, to the Vasco fans that day, farewell to the title that ended up being ours. We razzed those kids from São Januário. I was at the top, my name was mentioned everywhere, practically nominated to the National Team. Just now, that employee at the Maracanã Stadium entrance here, hi Anselmo, you're back? Hi, pal. Walking by. May I go in? Come on in, this is your home.

Fuck this traffic jam. I remembered the samba (*I wanna*

die, etc.) he had sung to Doctor Santos, he must have gone to Maracanã. I'm going there. Send an ambulance. *I wanna die during a great samba session,* it went, *to the beautiful sounds of a samba song.* My old friend explained that for a samba dancer it was glorious to die on the avenue parading for his Samba School. *I know I'm gonna die. I don't know what time, I will never forget Aurora my love.* My old buddy will never forget the son he hardly knows, his short lived glory days, everything he had and threw out the window. Auroras and Marias and Luzias, a lot of women passed through my friend's life. You'll never forget, right, old friend? What a fucking life. *I know I'm gonna die, I don't know what day, I will never forget Luzia my girl.* All the things he did and said, I already start missing them like crazy. Luzia or Maria? He went to Maracanã to say farewell to everything. I was sure right away, with the lyrics of the samba banging in my head, I remembered him, my old friend, making music by using a matchbox like a tambourine while he called the waiter: Pour it, my man. That's enough, buddy. To the last drop, he said, while the waiter was pouring out the bottle. And he laughed like a kid.

Home. Then, the first sip of *cachaça*, to run to the touchline, thirty, ninety times. That's where the happiness of a goal or a short pass to a teammate was. *The Farewell Waltz.* Is my friend in doubt that I can still run to the touchline? Then, you will see (another sip), you'll see, my friend. Where is my old buddy? The man who just talked to me wasn't him. Or was he? Pouring out the *cachaça* bottle and the crowds start to applaud, inside his head, he runs and gets tired, he stops and the fans start to curse him, and that's inside his head, and he sees the stadium employee in the distance (it's not my friend, no) scratching his head. He waved to the man, the only spectator, as he used to do to the crowds in the past. He heard laughter, hands clapping, fireworks cracking, the shouts, the boos, the cheers, the curses. Everything was mixed up now. Everything was inside his head, he was saying farewell, running to the touchline, dribbling (but there was nobody), breaking the defense (nobody), kicking (without the ball) to goal. Scoring a goal. Lots of goals. Maracanã Stadium, in total silence, empty. Only that man who looked at him in the distance and all of a sudden he can't focus on the man clearly, the man's figure disappearing, he only sees a small blur, disappearing, fading, getting smaller, and smaller, and smaller, fading, and smaller, and in the swirl inside his head all the voices faded and suddenly silence was the only thing he heard. At last, the long-awaited silence exploding.